*Praise for*

# The Time It Snowed in Puerto Rico

"Sarah McCoy has written a story so replete with sensuality, so infused with love and community, so exquisitely observant and poetic, the reader can only wish for a package tour to the dream that is Verdita's life."

— SANDRA SCOFIELD, author of *Opal on Dry Ground* and *Occasions of Sin*

"Sarah McCoy tells a story of magic, myth, and mystery amid political and cultural unrest. You can't help loving Verdita, the world she comes from, and the world she yearns for. A delightful debut by a promising and saucy new writer."

— SHERI REYNOLDS, author of *A Gracious Plenty*

"It is with the eye for color and detail of a master gardener that McCoy locates the fertile place space between the very precious and the wildly furious where the nature of the revelatory bildungsroman flourishes."

— H. G. CARRILLO, author of *Loosing My Espanish*

# The Time It Snowed in Puerto Rico

### A Novel

## Sarah McCoy

THREE RIVERS PRESS

NEW YORK

Copyright © 2009 by Sarah McCoy

Discussion Guide copyright © 2009 by Shaye Areheart Books, an imprint of the Crown Publishing Group, a division of Random House, Inc., New York.

All rights reserved.
Published in the United States by Three Rivers Press, an imprint of the Crown Publishing Group, a division of Random House, Inc., New York.
www.crownpublishing.com

THREE RIVERS PRESS and the Tugboat design are registered trademarks of Random House, Inc.

Originally published in hardcover in the United States by Shaye Areheart Books, an imprint of the Crown Publishing Group, a division of Random House, Inc., New York, in 2009.

Library of Congress Cataloging-in-Publication Data

McCoy, Sarah, 1980–
The time it snowed in Puerto Rico / Sarah McCoy.—1st ed.
1. Teenage girls—Fiction.  2. Adolescence—Fiction.
3. Puerto Rico—Fiction.  I. Title.
PS3613.C38573T56 2009
813'.6—dc22                2008051513

ISBN 978-0-307-46017-2

Printed in the United States of America

Design by Lauren Dong

10  9  8  7  6  5  4  3  2  1

First Paperback Edition

*For my Mommacita,*
*Eleane Norat McCoy*

# The Time It Snowed in
## Puerto Rico

*Chapter One*

May 1961

FOR MY ELEVENTH BIRTHDAY, PAPI MADE *PIRAGUAS*. He left balloons of water in the freezer until they were solid, then peeled the plastic off like bright banana skins. On the veranda, he used his machete to shave the globes into ice chips. Hard bits of cold spit out where the ball and blade met, landing on my arms and legs, cheeks and nose. Papi said it was a Puerto Rican snowfall, and laughed long and deep. Mamá and I did, too. She sat beside me under Papi's snow until we shivered and held each other close to warm back up.

After the balls were chiseled into a pile of white, we poured passionfruit syrup over it and ate right from the bowl. The sweet flakes made my mouth cold and itchy, and I had to suck my lips to warm my tongue. We couldn't eat it all, though; it turned to a puddle under the sun. Papi said snow did that, changed into everyday water. I'd never been in a snowfall before. I didn't know.

That night, the first heat wave of the season swept over the island and nobody could sleep. I lay in bed, the outside fever making my underwear dig into my skin and itch.

"Papi, tell me a story," I said. Miserable, I wanted the everyday to shift to dreams.

"You're too old for stories now. Why don't I read about Jacob and Isaac?" Mamá liked it best when he read from the Bible at bedtime. She believed it would help me dream good things. Papi took a seat in my bamboo chair. The ceiling fan clicked around around. "Or maybe Daniel in the lion's den?" He winked at me.

When I was little, I had a crush on the brave and mighty Daniel who played with lions. Mamá disapproved. She said that it wasn't right for someone to have romantic feelings for a dead man, never mind a dead holy man. Papi said it was better Daniel of the Bible than Roberto Confresi, the pirate.

"Can't I hear the story of my name?" I asked.

In Puerto Rico, everybody had two names. One was printed on a birth certificate. Another was the one you were called, the name you answered to, and that name always came with a story. Mamá's birth certificate said "Monaique." Papi's said "Juan." But nobody called them that because those names had no story.

They called Papi *Faro*, "Lighthouse," because as a child

he loved to watch the flashing light on Aguadilla Beach. My *abuela*, Mamá Juanita, said they often went to Aguadilla to visit her brother's family. On one particular visit, the family stayed up late listening to troubadour songs, and just before bed, Mamá Juanita noticed that Papi wasn't with the group. Everyone searched the house, but he was gone. Then, from the kitchen window, she saw a small, soft hump sitting outside on the beach rock. It was Papi. He stared out toward the sea, watching the lighthouse beam slice the black again and again. When she asked what he was doing, he said, "Keeping watch." Mamá Juanita called him Little Faro, and the nickname stuck.

They called my mamá Venusa because as a girl she nearly drowned while surfing the northwest coast of Puerto Rico. Papi told me how a wave rolled over and pulled her down to the coral bottom. The Ocean King saw her there, her black hair streaking the blue, and thought her so lovely that he decided to change her into a mermaid. The sea-weed wrapped her legs and the coral caged her. Mamá prayed for a miracle—to return to our island. Then, just when she thought her skin would change to scales, a rush of water pushed her from the King's prison, up through the blue-green, until her eyes saw the sun and her skin sparkled pink. She'd been gone so long that everyone believed her dead, lost to the ocean world. But she was reborn, like the goddess Venus.

Those were the stories we lived by. Who my parents were, who I was. My birth certificate said "Maria Flores

Ortiz-Santiago," but they called me Verdita. Papi kept all our certificates on the shelf in his study beside three dead roosters with black marble eyes. The names were as life-less as the cocks with their sawdust guts. Only our nick-names were alive. Papi told my story best.

He leaned back in the chair. "Venusa, Verdita wants to hear her story again."

From the kitchen where Mamá scrubbed the scales off codfish, she laughed. "She's like you. Head in the clouds." But I was glad to be like Papi. Mamá wasn't a good story-teller. She forgot parts or added things from the priest's sermons. Papi always remembered it right and always began the same way.

He closed the Bible. "Your story started long before you left your mamá's body, before you took your first breath. Your soul spoke to me from heaven."

I curled up my toes and closed my eyes, concentrating on Papi's words.

In a dream, Papi stood alone on a strange and colorful beach, unlike any in Puerto Rico. The ocean was unusu-ally calm, and the air was silent except for the lull of the breeze through the coconut palms. No lick of seaweed or burrow of crayfish—the sand sparkled in rainbow peb-bles. In the distance was Mamá, her wavy hair caught in the breeze, black against the light. Papi went to her.

I imagined the beach like the photograph I kept in the crack of my mirror. In it, Mamá stood between bright umbrellas and candy-colored towels, a beach carnival. Her head was thrown back, her mouth open, and I could hear laughter through the glossy paper. On the back was written *Visit to Orlando and Lita Virginia Beach, 1950*. It was taken just before she got pregnant with me, just before Papi had his dream.

He leaned forward in the chair. "And just as I reached her, I heard a burst of water. A sea spout lifted some fifty feet in the air. So high that I had to shield my eyes against the brightness of the sky and the white surf. I was afraid it was the Ocean King come for Venusa at last. But she turned and smiled. She knew what I didn't. From the top of the spout, a parrot with emerald feathers and two gleaming green eyes flew from the watery perch and landed on my shoulder."

I took a deep breath and held it.

"That was your spirit," Papi continued. "I have never seen such a beautiful bird on earth."

Papi leaned in and kissed my forehead. I could smell the soap and the little bit of Old Spice aftershave that he used so long ago, when the day was first born. I breathed him in.

In my story, Mamá had a handful of sesame seeds, and she fed them to the parrot until it was full. Then it took flight, spreading its emerald wings in the coconut breeze, up, up into the cloudless blue. It left behind a single green feather. Papi tucked it in the front of his shirt for safekeeping, but when he woke from the dream, it was gone.

"And I was searching the bed looking everywhere for

the feather when your mamá came into the room with a cup of *café con leche*. She asked me what I was doing, and I told her that I had lost something important. That's when she told me she was going to have a baby. You were inside her. And I knew the parrot in my dream was you."

At this point in my story, I always got sleepy. My sheets hugged my body; my pillow cupped my head. I closed my eyes but listened still.

"I told your mamá about the dream and she agreed. God must have put me on the shore of heaven so you could come to us."

I buried my face deeper into the darkness.

"The day you were born, I walked outside our house and noticed the whoosh of the breeze through the palms, just like in my dream. Mamá's water broke. She was in labor. We thought you were a boy at first—all the troubles she had. I had to take her to the hospital in San Juan because the *barrio* midwife was busy delivering two other children, and I knew she could not deliver alone.

"I sat outside of the operating room, waiting and watching for the doctor. Those were dark hours. But then a nurse came and took me to you. When I held you that first time, you opened your eyes and looked into mine. Big green eyes. *Verde*. Just like the parrot. And I knew we had met before. My Verdita."

Sleep washed over me like one of the waves on Papi's dream beach, soft and soundless.

I WOKE LATER to the slow hum of our radio singing out a *plena* song of a lovesick *jíbaro*. Papi was gone. It was still night, but a pink-yellow light glowed outside my bedroom like the candlelit halo of the Madonna at church. Pushing myself out of bed, my arms and legs moved slowly, as if I were still swimming in sleepy waters. I made my way from the darkness to the doorway, reaching out to touch the speckles of light, trying to cup the glow in my hands. It trickled through my fingers. I followed the lamplight to the living room. There, on the couch, were Papi and Mamá. I barely recognized them. He was shirtless. She wore only the bottom portion of her slip, her back brown and bare. Papi clasped her one hand against his chest. With his other, he rubbed the small of her back, round and round, to the music's pulse. They seemed to be dancing, but lying down and slower than I had ever seen before. It reminded me of how the priests looked when they prayed the graces necessary for salvation. These went on so long that old Señora Juarez always fell asleep, dropped her fan, and drooled. Mamá said they were praying themselves into heaven and if I closed my eyes and did as they did, I might be able to do the same. Mamá and Papi's bodies were there, but their spirits had risen to a place I could not see.

Their hips swayed back and forth to the voice of the *jíbaro* that lost his love, and to the twang of the guitar strings. Papi's face was lost beneath the dark waves of Mamá's mermaid hair. She had stolen him, swept him under her ocean. Their spirits swam to some depth that I could not reach, and I couldn't speak to bring them back, couldn't close my eyes to join them; my stare burned in the lamplight. I tried to walk away, but my legs grew roots. I stood silent, alone, and terrified, and I wondered if that was how hell felt.

A thick lock of Mamá's hair swung from her shoulder. I could see Papi's eyes, closed at first and then open. He saw me. "Verdita," he said to Mamá.

She turned, her cheeks pink and shiny with sweat. "Go!" she yelled, and covered her chest. "Leave!"

I ripped my legs from their roots and ran to bed, covered my head with the sheets, and said Hail Marys over and over. It was the only prayer I could remember. But even the Virgin Mary couldn't stop the music from humming. So I tried to think of something else—something good.

Under the sheets, I stared at the pink polka-dot buds on the cotton. The print reminded me of the dress Mamá just finished sewing. I'd picked out the exact pattern I wanted—a Simplicity with a blond girl on the cover wearing a small, blue-flower print dress. Bluebonnets, Mamá said. I'd never seen bluebonnets before. I searched the fabric store for hours looking for the same material, but Mamá said they only sold it in the States, and besides, she thought those flowers were ugly. Not like any of our island flowers. She liked the coral blooms best, young *magas* on the stem, and bought the whole bolt to sew matching dresses, though hers had simple pleats around the waist and mine was belled for a crinoline slip. When Papi saw us in them, side by side, for the first time, he put his hand to his forehead: "*Ay! Muy bonita!* I have the two most beautiful girls on the island!" It had felt good to be seen that way—beautiful, like Mamá. But not now. The memory made me sick.

I pulled the sheet off my head to breathe. The dress hung in the closet. I shut my eyes to keep from seeing it. I never wanted to wear it. Never. I wanted something else— bluebonnets like the girls in the United States. When I grew up, I swore I'd go there and leave all this behind.

IN THE MORNING, my voice was back, my legs unstuck. So I decided to bounce my lime-colored ball on the bedroom tiles, counting each as loudly as possible, snapping the silence with each throw.

"One!" The ball bounced. "Two!" It bounced again. "Three! Four! Five!" I counted. The sound of the rubber springing against the floor vibrated the walls of our pink house. I wanted Mamá and Papi to know I was awake— wanted them to wake up too. Their bedroom door was closed. So I took my bouncy ball out onto the tiles of the living room, walking past the couch, being sure not to look at it. I flicked on the radio. A fast *bomba* played, and I bounced to its rhythm. I didn't hear the front door swing open.

Mamá entered, fully dressed, her hair pinned up in a knot, carrying a bowl of brown eggs. She'd been up for hours already, or maybe she'd never slept at all. She didn't say anything, just turned the radio down as she passed on her way to the stove. I didn't really want to talk to *her*, but I wanted to talk. So I asked, "Where's Papi?" without looking at her or breaking the steady beat of rebounding rubber.

"*Allí*," she said and motioned with her nose toward the veranda.

Outside, Papi swung his machete, splitting coconuts; a stack of five or six lay at his feet.

"Coconut milk, again? I bet Omar gets to have real milk in Washington, D.C. Wish I was with him. Not here on this stupid *finca*, this stupid island," I said, and immediately wondered where the words came from.

Omar was my cousin. Tío Orlando and Titi Lita moved to the States when he was still cutting his teeth on sugarcane. In the summers they sent him back to visit because they said he was forgetting Puerto Rico. It was true.

The summer before, he'd asked me during breakfast if we had any cereal. "*Sí*, we have *con-flei*," I'd said, and pointed with my nose to the cabinet.

"Huh? What's that?"

Everybody knew what that was. I shook my head and motioned again with my lips for added emphasis, the way Mamá did. He stared back at me without moving.

"*Ay bendito!*" I opened the cabinet. "*Con-flei* is sugar

flakes and Lucky Charms." I said it slowly and in perfect English so he'd understand. I didn't tell him that the same box of Lucky Charms had been there since the *Navidad*. A line of dots marched to and from it even now. Sugar ants. It was a wonder they hadn't nibbled all the bits inside.

Mamá didn't move in the kitchen. It must have been a shock for her to hear me talk that way. I'd never done it in the past. Her back was to me, so I couldn't see her face. She cracked an egg into the bowl. It crumbled in her fist. Without speaking, she picked the shells out of the yolk, and I noticed how pale the skin on the back of her neck looked, hidden beneath so much dark hair. I wondered if I was hidden from the light for long enough, if my skin would turn white like that, like the girl on the cover of the Simplicity pattern. Colorless, like the jelly of an egg. I loved and hated that foreign skin; it didn't match mine.

Papi came in when the eggs were fried. He set the jug of fresh coconut milk on the breakfast table, and I wished I could take back what I'd said about it. His forehead was beaded with sweat from cracking the thick shells and strain-ing the juice.

"*Buenos días*, Verdita." He kissed the top of my head and then Mamá's cheek. The same cheek that had been flushed and slick the night before. Now it was dry and smeared with rouge. She ran her thin fingers over his hand, and I thought they looked like spiders crawling over the dead.

"Verdita isn't really my name," I said. Papi turned from Mamá to face me. "If I lived in the States, they'd make you call me what it says on my birth certificate. Maria Flores. They'd make you."

Mamá turned too. They looked at me, and Papi scrunched the skin on his forehead so that the sweat beads ran together down the middle arch between his eyebrows. He thumbed the trickle away.

I wished I could take back all my words from that day. Verdita was my name. I had *my* story, and I loved coconut milk.

Suddenly I felt nauseated. The eggs on the table smelled of pork grease and butchered chicks. I thought I was going to throw up.

"Verdita." Papi took a firm seat at the table; the silverware tinkled with his weight. "Sit down and eat your breakfast."

I sat. Mamá sat next to me, and we all bowed our heads to thank God for the food. I prayed that whatever they prayed wouldn't pray them into heaven and leave me there alone. And then I prayed as hard as I could, squinting until my eyes ached, that I could turn back into an emerald parrot and fly to heaven or find the Ocean King and become his mermaid—I'd take either. When I opened my eyes, they were still sitting there, and I hadn't sprouted wings or a fishtail. I tried to swallow the slippery fried egg, but it nearly came back up.

After breakfast, Papi asked if I wanted to walk down

the road to buy sesame seed bars while he talked to his friends about the local news. I knew what he was trying to do: trick me into trusting him again—into forgetting the night before. I wouldn't fall for it.

"I got schoolwork," I said, even though I didn't. "A paper."

"A paper? School's almost finished for summer, *verdad*?" Papi asked.

"It's the last one. I have to write about—about myself," I lied.

"What about yourself?"

"Just who I am. Teachers always want us to write stories about who we are."

I tried not to look him in the eyes. I'd never lied to him before, and I knew I wasn't good at it. I grabbed a pencil and notebook and went out on the veranda.

*Odio. Odio. Odio.* I hate. I hate. I hate. I wrote in Spanish and English, just to keep my pencil moving fast. Then I switched it up. *Maria Flores Ortiz-Santiago*. I wrote my official name again and again until it became strange to look at, the letters nothing more than lines and dots. Maria Flores. To be able to live with Juan and Monaique, maybe that's who I needed to be.

Papi walked out the back door and down the driveway, then turned to me. "I'll see you later."

I nodded, like I was too busy to say anything. But I liked that Papi was trying. So maybe I wouldn't hate him as much. I'd just hate Mamá. In my mind, I saw her over and over—barebacked, flushed and slick against Papi; her voice still echoed. "Go. Leave." My stomach turned.

*V-e-r-d-i-t-a.* I wrote slowly across the top of the page. *Verdita.* I read it to myself, the familiar *r* rolling off my tongue. I wanted my nickname story to fill me up, but worried that it never would again.

*Chapter Two*

# Dare

THAT SUMMER, WHEN THE COQUI MATING CHIRPS grew so loud I could barely sleep, Omar came to visit. I couldn't wait for him to arrive, but when he did, I noticed he'd changed too. The summer before, our arm muscles and feet and hands had matched each other, and we'd both liked to run and climb to the same spot on our *ceiba* tree where the branches widened and neither one of us could reach any higher. We were equals then, but now his fingers and toes stretched long and full, like *morcilla* sausages; he could outrun and outclimb me, and he did it every chance he got.

Papi said that Omar was becoming a man, and took him out on the *finca* a few times. He even let Omar use the machete to crack coconuts. Papi never let me do that. I wasn't allowed anywhere near the toolshed. It made me burning mad.

Omar thought he was better than me, because he was older and a boy and had been to the States. I'd never left the island. He said he'd seen things in Washington, D.C., that would make me cry for my mamá and try to swim back to Puerto Rico. He'd seen a homeless man who froze to death during a snowstorm. They found his iced body on a street near the White House, where the president lived. I'd felt snow and could imagine freezing. But I told Omar, "So what?" even though I shivered at the thought of a dead man. I'd never seen one of those.

He told me about a place called Anaconda, a town of snakes. He'd never been, but my *tío* told stories about men who lived there and murdered each other for red devils and juice. Snake poisons, Omar said. There weren't any poisonous snakes in Puerto Rico. He had me with that one. But no matter how much Omar had seen, I wasn't going to let him get away with being all high and mighty.

Omar brought something else new with him. A game he said that everybody in the States played. It was called "Dare." We didn't have Dare in Puerto Rico, or at least not in Florilla, our *barrio*. But I was a quick learner.

"So, you up to the challenge?" he asked.

"Are you?" I said.

He'd spent a good half hour huffing and puffing over the rules of Dare, even though I got them all in the first five minutes. Basically, you made up things for the other person to do, and they had to do them or else be a coward—a chicken.

"We got to flip a coin to see who goes first. I call heads." He pulled a quarter from his pocket and spun it in the air. It clinked tails on the tile floor. Omar smirked like he knew something I didn't. I was tired of everybody thinking they knew something I didn't.

"Dare me," he said.

I was ready. The three dead roosters in Papi's study were stiff and old. I might have thought of them as dolls, maybe even played with them, except that the skin on their claws was cold and goosebumped, and sometimes, out of the corner of my eye, I could see them move. But of course they kept still when I turned to look straight on. Ever since we were little, we'd made up spirit tales about those cocks. No matter how grown-up Omar was, I knew he still believed in some things.

"I dare you to stay locked in the study with the dead roosters for ten minutes." I eyed the clock in the hallway.

Omar coughed like a laugh stuck in his throat, like it was no big thing. But I knew it was.

"Fine," he said, and walked into the study without blinking.

I held the door open for him. "See you in ten minutes. I hope." I shook my head and sighed. "*Adiós*, Omar." I shut the door. The metal key stuck out of the lock like the roosters' stiff, dead tongues; I turned it and watched the clock tick-tock.

After five minutes, I put my ear to the door and listened. I could hear the clicking of Omar's fingers. He did that when he got nervous. I bit my lip to keep the excitement from squealing out. I liked him being afraid when I wasn't.

He'd been in there seven minutes when he cleared his throat. I stared hard at the doorknob; inside, I knew that the roosters were winking and moving toward him in the blurs. He cleared his throat again.

"Verdita?" There was a sudden bang. "Verdita, you better not cheat me. How long has it been?" He banged harder with his fist.

"Not yet time," I said. "But if you want to be a chicken, I can let you out."

Silence. That got him.

A few moments later, he rattled the doorknob. "Okay. Now?" It was only eight minutes.

"Nope," I said.

"Liar! Open the door, Verdita!"

"I'm not a——" I began, but before I had a chance to defend myself, Omar yelled, "Let me out!" His voice had reached that pitch—that one just before tears.

Even though I was safe outside, my stomach jumped. I quickly turned the key and pulled open the door. He rushed out, breathless, and I slammed the door behind him, protecting us from the monsters. It was fun to be scared, but only when you could control when it started and when it stopped.

"You kept me in there longer than ten minutes!" he said.

"*Ocho*." I smiled. "You lost."

"Only eight! Did you time it right?"

"*Sí*, look for yourself." I pointed toward the hallway clock.

"You cheated. That felt longer."

I shrugged and grinned. "No. *Mire*, the clock." Time couldn't lie, even if we could.

"Fine. Now it's my turn to dare," he said. "*You* stay in there for ten minutes."

I hadn't anticipated this. My palms went sweaty, but I wasn't about to let on. I turned the knob and entered, eyeing the roosters on the shelf, daring them to move. Omar shut the door behind me.

The first few minutes were easy. I took a seat on the floor, sucking and picking at my fingernails, cleaning the bits of green papaya rind from beneath. As I finished my left pinky, the first blurry shadow shifted. Turning my head up to the dead trio, I willed them to move when I could see, and at the same time my heart sped up, afraid that they actually would.

"*Gallos estúpidos*," I whispered.

Getting angry helped. I wouldn't let them scare me. It wasn't my fault they were dead—that they were weak and lost their fights. Cockfighting was the national sport of Puerto Rico. My whole life I'd seen weekly posters tacked to the walls of the stores in town. Papi only talked with his friends about the fights. And just that summer he'd asked Omar if he wanted to go with him to one. He didn't ask

Mamá or me. She told me it was a blood sport for men only, but I wanted to go. Papi put ten-dollar bills inside an old razor case in his room, and whenever there was a cock-fight, the money disappeared. Mamá didn't know.

He used to raise fighting roosters, but stopped when Tío Orlando moved to the States. He said he couldn't train any winners without him. Occasionally I'd see Papi in the study alone, dusting the dead with a cloth, running his fingers slowly over their feathers. They were his prize cocks—won every fight but their last. Mamá said it was God's will that the roosters died and Tío moved. Gambling was a terrible sin. We were Catholics, but I didn't think gam-bling was so wrong. Not like murder or adultery. Papi said he only watched the sport now.

At the edge of my vision, a rooster moved its head. I stopped breathing. Sweat trickled down my sides. With the door closed, the air felt thick and hot, like inhaling a bowl of *asopao* soup. I closed my eyes and tried to remem-ber the Christmas *parrandas*, the smell of the gardenia bush in the front yard, my *abuelo*'s tobacco-stained hands on mine, anything but the unblinking black eyes that I knew were watching me.

There was a scrape up along the ceiling ridge. They were coming, their stiff wings batting the air just behind my head, and I turned in circles trying to face them, to catch a glimpse. Panic tightened my chest. I imagined the hallway clock, tried to read it through the door. I had to beat Omar!

There was another creak. This time in the wooden shelving. I put my hands over my ears. Then I thought I saw something swift and dark move across the small, high window above the desk. I stood, my breath coming quickly, my eyes watering.

"Omar!" I pounded on the door. "How long?" I waited a moment, my hand on the knob, my stomach cramping. He didn't answer. "Omar!" I screamed louder and banged with my fist. There was only silence. No click of the key. No rattle of the knob.

"Help me! Omar! Open!"

The roosters were coming for me. Their stiff feathers brushed the back of my neck, their claws tangled my hair.

*"Por favor!"* My voice broke and I slid to my knees, staring into the dark keyhole. "Omar! Please, open the door!" I bit my lip to hold in the screams. I didn't care anymore how long it had been. I just wanted out.

"Papi!" I yelled.

Then, from the other side, a giggle.

I slammed my fists against the door and swore to myself that I'd knock it down if I had to. The key clicked, and Omar leaned in with a grin. I rushed at him and shoved all my panic right into his gut. He fell backwards on the concrete, and I stood over him. His eyes were wide.

"I was just playing around, Verdita," he said, and I could hear it in his voice: he was scared of me.

I didn't say a word. Instead, I left him there, next to the study where the roosters' ghosts were climbing back onto their stiff perches. I opened the door to the veranda. The hall clock chimed the hour.

I'd get him back.

EVEN WITH OMAR there, things were strained between Mamá and me. I tried not to talk to her at all. That was easy. I just spoke English. She didn't understand. It was a language only Papi, Omar, and I shared, and that suited me perfect. For a little bit she tried to learn, using words that Omar taught her: "Verdita, please." "Verdita, come." "Verdita, need." But I didn't want her to learn, so I laughed at her pronunciation and told her in Spanish that she was saying it all wrong, even though she wasn't. I did that until she finally gave up. I told Omar to stop teaching her or I'd put hot peppers in his bed.

When Mamá spoke to me in Spanish, I answered in English. It made her so mad. She stomped around in a stream of *Ay, Dios Mio*-es and pleas to God to help her deal with her burdens. I ignored her. Papi was working on the *finca* a lot and staying out late at the *jíbaros* bar, talking politics. When he was home, I played innocent, pretending not to understand why Mamá was so upset. She insisted I was misbehaving and should be punished, but I made my eyes real big and said, "No, Papi. I've been good." I even sounded more "good" in English. Papi, confused, simply threw up his hands and said he didn't understand women.

Then he told me, "I have my eye on you," and it made me nervous because I knew he did.

One afternoon the heat forced Omar and me outside, where there was a little bit of an island breeze. Omar pulled out the dominoes and lined them up on their ends. There was nothing else to do, so I helped him. But after a while I got bored with the lines of black and white dots, their neat rows forming mazes on the terra-cotta tiles.

"Hey," I whispered. The windows were open to the kitchen, where Mamá was already making a *mixto arroz con pollo* for dinner. Olive oil and cilantro *sofrito* simmer-ing with the chicken in the pot. It made me hungry. "You want to get some sesame seed candy at the bar?" I asked Omar, and jingled the coins in my pocket. The *jíbaros* bar down the road sold it, but Papi forbade us to go there.

Of all the stuff Omar forgot about Puerto Rico, he hadn't forgotten Papi's rules. "Tío Faro said we can't."

Obviously he only forgot the everyday stuff, like that you *eat* the slippery seeds in passionfruit, you don't spit them out, and of course, what *con-flei* was. Sometimes I wondered if he was just pretending, but couldn't under-stand why anybody would do that.

"I dare you."

"Tío said no."

"I know. *Pero, stoy aburrido,*" I whined.

"Huh? What'd you say?"

"This is *boring*," I repeated in English, and pushed over a domino, sending a part of his column into a cascade.

"Ay! Verdita! I was setting them up."

I stood and kicked over the rest. "*Careculo.*" Buttface.

"What did you call me?" Omar asked.

"What? You forgot your name? *Ay Dios mio, lo siento.*"

"Maybe I'll just go inside and ask Titi Venusa what you said."

Through the horizontal window slats, slivers of Mamá moving around the kitchen gathering ingredients for supper. "*Mamagüero,*" I whispered under my breath.

"You suck balls too," said Omar.

"Oh! You *do* know what I'm saying. I'm glad to see you're remembering again."

Down the gravel road from our house, the Lopezes' purple-painted home bordered the tarred main street. Señora Lopez had just finished peeling her plantains on the porch and had gone inside. There was no one around to see us. Omar stood up and followed my gaze. "Candy, huh?"

"*Sí.* Sometimes Papi brings sesame bars home when he stops for a drink after work. It's the best. Better than the stuff we buy in town. Crunchy. Sweet." I almost had him. "And, you know, I dared you."

The brown edges of his eyes glinted gold.

"They don't have them in D.C.," Omar admitted. "Well, not the good kind. There's one Latino store that sells them, but they're always stale."

"Stale!" I shook my head for effect. "Not ours. They're fresh here."

"Okay. I'll take your dare."

I knew he would.

After checking to make sure Mamá was still busy stirring and chopping, Omar and I jumped off the porch and sprinted toward the street. We didn't look back or speak or stop to breathe until we rounded the bend and my pink house was nowhere to be seen. Then we stopped, gulped in the humid air, and relished the panic in our chests.

"Think she saw us?" Omar asked.

I shook my head. "We'd have heard her by now if she had." Mamá could yell my name across the whole *barrio* if she put her mind to it, especially if she saw us running in the direction of the bar. "I think we're safe, but we got to hurry."

We had to walk single file along the crooked roads of our mountain town. Though two-way, the street was just wide enough for a single car. Tangled, wet bush framed the unmarked tar. The thick vines curled around the tree trunks like plaits of wet hair. I led the way. We couldn't talk because I had to listen for cars rounding the curves. From walking with Mamá to buy loaves of *pan de agua*, I had an ear for the coming whine of an engine making its fast climb up the tilted streets. When I heard it, I knew I had less than five seconds to move off the road into the bush. I stopped and gave Omar a push to his chest. "Get back. *Cheby* coming."

"What? I don't see anything," Omar said, but the whirring and grinding of gears came closer. I pushed him into a poinciana tree. The prickly blossoms stuck hard. "Ow! Verdita!"

A car zoomed past. The air seemed to collect the hot dust and brush it brown over my skin. Island dirt, it stained me as much as the sun.

"Told you," I said, and continued. Omar's eyes looked like they did when I unlocked the study door after hearing him pound and scream.

We went on. A few early coquis began to sing. *Co-qui, co-qui, co-qui.* It was a slow song by a handful of frogs. I wondered what time it was. I'd forgotten to look at the clock before we left. Five o'clock? Six, maybe? We usually ate at seven; the rice was already on the stove. Sweat beaded on my upper lip, and I licked the salt away. If we were late for supper, I'd get the belt for sure, but I'd make sure Omar got half the spanks. I'd remind Papi that he was older and a boy.

The *jíbaros* bar had a red neon sign above the door that said Schlitz. The bulb of the *l* had gone out at some point, so for as long as I could remember, the sign said Schitz, which I knew was a bad word on the mainland. Shits. I used it around Mamá because she didn't know "shits" from "sheets," but Papi was a different story. This is shits, I said once when Mamá made me wash the banana leaves for the *pasteles*. Papi heard and spanked me hard with his belt folded in half. I made sure never to say it again in front of him. I turned to Omar. "This place is the shits."

He didn't laugh, so I laughed for him.

That night there were so many cars parked outside that a few burrowed holes right into the jungle bush. Stacks of candy stood by the counter just inside the bar's open doorway: *dulces de ajonjolí, batata, coco-leche,* and *naranja.* My mouth watered. As we entered, I dug deep in my pocket for the coins.

"Look," Omar whispered.

The bar was packed full of men standing in a circle, their faces twisted in jagged smiles and squinty eyes. The loud cries of "Kill him!" and "Hit him again!" made something inside my stomach cramp. The men drank from small silver beer cans that fit snugly in their palms and looked like hand grenades I had seen in the movies. Their shouts and gazes were fixed on something in the middle of the circle. And while they screamed for blood, it was different from the angry feeling I got when the older boys at school fist-fought. It felt like that moment when the study lock clicked open after sitting with the dead.

"Come on." I pulled on Omar's arm, but he didn't move. I wanted to see what they saw, but didn't want to go alone. "You too scared?" His body slowly shifted forward.

We pushed into the crowd. In the center of the *gallera,* two roosters rolled in the dust, covered in black ooze, and pocked with holes in their feathers. Strange pieces of metal tied to their feet gave them ghoulish, bloody claws. They sprang into the air, aiming the spurs at each other. The eyeball of one swung on its purple-blue thread. The comb atop the other's brow was completely torn off. A rainbow of feathers stuck to blood clots and matted the concrete.

The men's laughter popped the air like bubbles rising in a boiling soup. Then, across the circle, I saw him—Papi. He sat with a handful of men, cards in his hand, green bills piled high. He crushed a cigar into the table ledge, looked up, and our eyes met. I couldn't run or hide or look away. The men around the *gallera* cheered in low growls; wings beat hard against the heat; spurs splintered bone; bodies moved in dark shadows. Papi started toward us, but the circle of men and the fighting roosters stood between.

Omar pulled my arm. He yanked hard, but my legs wouldn't move. "Come!" he shouted above the men's voices.

I didn't follow. The roosters jumped and pecked, clawed and bled. I couldn't stop watching.

Then Papi squeezed my shoulder. "What are you doing here?"

"We wanted candy."

"Is Omar with you?" he asked.

*"Allí."* I motioned my nose toward the door. Papi didn't say another word. I'd get the belt for sure. But I wanted it—the familiar sting. I wanted to hear the belt clap down hard on my skin so I could hush the rushing wings, the crunching of spurs against bone.

Outside, Omar sat on the dirt, his back against an old

Chevy with muddy wheels and missing hubcaps. His face shone slick and pale.

Papi put a firm hand on each of our shoulders. "Get in the car."

We climbed into his jeep and drove up the winding mountain road in silence. I wondered what would happen to the rooster that lost the fight. Who washed the bloody marks off the floor? Who stuffed the body with wood chips and put marbles in the eyes? I wondered if Papi's hands were stained red. Red like the playing cards that he had held. Omar put his hand on mine. I clenched my fists and turned to look out the window. Papi parked in front of our house. Through the window, Mamá moved around the kitchen, laying out plates.

"*Hola querido!*" she said when she saw Papi. "What's this?" She nodded toward us.

"Go to my study," Papi instructed. His dark eyes were ringed red.

Omar and I obeyed. We sat in the study, side by side, looking down at the floor. Papi didn't scare me as much as the three dead roosters winking and the flood of images from the *jíbaros* bar. In the kitchen, Mamá chattered and scraped the crusty *pegao* from the bottom of the rice pot. It reminded me of the roosters' spurs as they landed and dragged their feet on the concrete. I put my hands over my ears and closed my eyes, but even there I could still see Papi and the ring of men, even clearer.

"Verdita!" Papi shook me by the shoulder. He sat in

his wooden study chair and leaned forward so close that I saw the wide, shiny pores on his nose, smelled the steel of grenades on his breath. "What do you want? You can have the belt or we can talk about what you did wrong. It's your choice."

This was how my papi punished, with choices. But I knew better. *We* didn't talk. Papi talked and talked and yelled and talked. The belt was quicker. Pain for only a moment and then it was done.

Before Omar had a chance to say anything, I spoke up. "The belt."

Omar shook his head, but it had been decided. Papi unhooked his belt, folded it in half, and thumbed the leather.

"Verdita, I told you not to go there," Papi said.

"*Lo siento,*" I whispered. And I really was.

"Get up."

We did.

"Omar, leave us," he said.

Omar's entire body jumped a little. Then he took off down the hall.

"You won't go there again." Papi stood. His arms flexed, ready to swing. I squeezed the cheeks of my *culito*, antici‹ pating the sting, and mad that Omar wasn't there beside me. Papi pushed a hand through his hair; his tobacco‹ stained hands ran over the belt edge. Then he touched the top of my head.

"Go. Dinner is waiting."

I walked from the study to the dining room table and took a seat with Omar and Mamá. It was a while before Papi joined us. Mamá didn't speak or sing or hum or move while we waited for him, and neither did we. When he finally did come, his belt was looped back around his waist and he didn't say another word about the *jíbaros* bar or the roosters. Instead, he blessed our meal and talked of the day and the sugarcane and the heat; then he drank a Schlitz, laughed, and kissed Mamá for her good cooking. Omar smiled so big it hurt my gums to watch. He asked for second helpings of Mamá's rice and said *gracias*-this and *gracias*-that. They all went on like nothing had happened, like they'd been to the States and forgotten. But I knew. I remembered it all. I could barely eat my plateful, even though my stomach growled and cramped. The *mixta* tasted like copper, red saffron-stained rice and cooked chicken flesh. I picked a small wingbone from the pile of rice on my plate.

## Chapter Three

# Gringo Elvis

In the winter, the rains came. Stuck inside our schoolroom, nobody could concentrate. At first I thought it had something to do with the *Navidad* and the *Día de Reyes* and the coming holiday break. But the conversations weren't about *parrandas* and presents, fireworks and troubadours, not even about the rain.

It wasn't just the students, either. The teachers huddled in the halls, their voices tinkled like broken bells. At home, Papi's friends from the *jíbaros* bar came over in the evenings to complain about the weather and debate politics over glasses of gin. Everybody was talking about the United States, President Kennedy, and Puerto Rican statehood.

One night during dinner, Papi pulled the television close to the table so he could watch the news. Parts were in English. Mamá didn't like it. She cleared her throat and hummed aloud, so Papi turned up the volume.

"What's the big deal with President Kennedy?" I asked. The news showed a photograph of the smiling president and his smiling wife surrounded by children waving American flags, all smiling.

*"Para! El público!"* The newscaster spoke every word as an exclamation. "Come! See! The American! President!"

"He's coming," said Papi. He leaned back in his chair and tossed a half-eaten drumstick onto his plate. I nibbled on the tough skin of my sweet-and-sour chicken thigh. Mamá had overcooked the meat and burned the rice. She'd been mindless all day.

I set the thigh to the side and licked my sticky fingers one by one. Mamá handed me a napkin. Copper fingerprints stained the white.

"To our *barrio?*" I crumpled the napkin in my fist and sucked my saucy thumb. Mamá frowned, but I pretended not to notice. "Why?" There was nothing but corn, tobacco, and jungle for miles. Nothing a president would be interested in.

Mamá hummed louder. Papi turned up the volume again.

"No. To San Juan," Papi explained. "On December fifteenth. He's flying here to meet Governor Muñoz Marín. For sure, it will be one big fiesta."

"Can we go, Papi? Are we going to be an American state?"

"Maybe. Many want us to. Many don't." He laid his palm firmly on the table, our glasses shook.

"Do you want us to become a state?" I asked.

But Mamá cleared her throat. "Politicians are nothing but gamblers—they use words instead of cards. Faro, please, not at dinner, not with Verdita," she said.

"I like politics." I licked another finger. Heat prickled up from my belly. If Papi and I wanted to talk politics, so be it. Mamá could just keep her nose out of that, too. And besides, she didn't know a thing about it. This wasn't just politics—this was important! Plenty of other United States presidents had come to play golf and vacation, but normal people, like me, weren't allowed to see them. They only printed photographs in the newspaper after they left. But now there was going to be a public fiesta in San Juan, and the whole island was invited.

Mamá sighed. "I'm sick of hearing these men talk, talk, talk." She spooned her rice. "Besides, I have news of my own."

Papi turned down the television.

I rolled my eyes. It was just like her to try to change the subject.

"I had an appointment with Dr. Lopez today," she said.

Papi cocked his head and sucked his teeth. *"Sí?"*

Mamá's eyes twinkled wet; she sucked her bottom lip and nodded.

"No!" Papi's eyes went big as eggs. "Are you? Did we?" He rose from his seat and nearly knocked the television over.

I looked from him to Mamá, confused. They spoke a secret language, some code I hadn't learned. Did they *what*?

"Ah-ha!" Papi laughed. "It's a miracle!" He lifted Mamá off her chair and kissed her.

I twisted my paper napkin to shreds. "What's going on?"

"I'm going to have a baby." Mamá laughed.

"A baby!" repeated Papi.

Suddenly I seemed to slip underwater. The sounds echoed, the lamplight marbled while they hugged and kissed. I was watching it all, but wasn't a part of it. Mamá was going to have a baby? I knew she'd wanted one for years, but I'd overheard Titi Lola say she couldn't, so I figured it was true—figured I was safe.

The sweet-and-sour taste caught in my throat. I definitely didn't want Mamá to have a boy. Papi would love a boy more than me. Everybody did. He'd have a son to take to the cockfights and work on the *finca* and talk English with. He wouldn't need me. But if Mamá had a girl— and she was beautiful—Mamá and Papi would definitely love her more. I hated it, the baby, whatever it was. And I despised them for making it.

I left them in the kitchen, went to my room, and shut the door. I thought my head would burst. Everything was changing so fast. I crawled underneath my sheets and closed my eyes, trying to dream my way back to Papi's perfect rainbow beach. I was nearly there when the door creaked open and a beam of light pierced the darkness.

"Verdita," whispered Mamá, silhouetted in the door-way. *"Querida?"*

I ignored her.

"She's asleep," said Papi. He ran his hand over her belly. "She's happy."

But I wasn't. I was wide awake and couldn't seem to find my dreams again, no matter how hard I tried.

WE HAD MUSIC class the next morning, so I let myself forget about the night before. Music and English reading were my favorites. I got to show everybody how good my English was. Words changed during those hours. Everything sounded like magic. Our teacher, Señora Alonzo, was good at both singing and reading. She had a nice voice and could play the mandolin. Papi said she was born in New York City but was still a Puerto Rican; she had island blood even though her body was in the States. There were rumors she'd sung in an American band. Words rolled off her tongue like music. I hoped she never stopped teaching, but if she did, I thought she'd make a good casino singer or a priest, if priests could be girls. Mass would be so much better if she was reading the scripture. Señora Alonzo was the first woman teacher in Florilla, the first American too, and I loved her best of all.

That morning we sang the Puerto Rican national anthem, "La Borinqueña." That was one of my favorites. It said that our island, Borínquen, was a beautiful woman, the daughter of the ocean and the sun, who had a body covered in flowers. And knowing what I knew—what Papi told me about the Ocean King wanting Mamá—I imagined the song was my own. I pretended I was Borínquen. And sometimes, in the middle of the chorus, I'd truly believe.

After we finished our anthem, we sang the United States anthem. We always started music class with both. The daily songs were written in white chalk on the green board: *La Borinqueña, The Star-Spangled Banner, Class Choice.* Señora Alonzo strummed the opening melody on her mandolin.

" 'The Star-Spangled Banner.' *Uno, dos, tres.*"

We began to sing, hesitating at each line, trying to follow her sweet sound.

Ohhh sé con yoo sí bi de donsair leelite. We sang together. A few of the girls giggled, stumbling through the words.

*"Bueno!"* Señora Alonzo said at the end. "We'll practice this again. Okay. What else do we want to sing today? The last song is a class choice."

"Let's twiss again!" Mikal yelled.

"Besame la Bemba," Fredo shouted next to me.

"Will you love me tomorrow!"

"It's Now o' Never!" said Sonia two rows over.

"Ay! Elvis Presley! How many like Elvis? I like Elvis." Señora Alonzo's eyes sparkled. We all raised our hands and made "oo*oo" sounds. I didn't feel one way or another about Elvis, but I did love Señora Alonzo. If she liked Elvis, then I liked Elvis. I raised my arm like a needle to the sky.

"*Perfecto!*" She smiled wide, and giggles rippled over the classroom. "It's Now or Never." She strummed the man*dolin.

"Ready, class? *Uno, dos, tres.*" She sang. I joined my voice to hers, my sound drowning in the group. I liked the way it felt. The rhythm was familiar and yet not. That's how a lot of music from the States felt. Something deep down in the chords made you want to move, to dance, but in a different way than our *jíbaros* songs. The songs from the States made me want to run, to jump, to spin until all the colors of the room blurred together. And at the same time they scared me so bad that I had to stop singing and hold my breath until the feeling passed. I did so then, and noticed that Fredo wasn't singing either.

Señora Alonzo strummed the last of the chorus, "My love won't wait." She looked in our direction and set the mandolin beside her chair. "Verdita. Fredo. Why don't you sing with the class? *Por qué?*"

Fredo stared straight, his eyes bulging wide and un*afraid. He looked the way Papi did when I talked back to him about my name and when he found me at the *jíbaros* bar. "My papá says that's a *gringo* song. I'm not allowed to sing *gringo* songs." I couldn't hold back my gasp, and I covered my own mouth for Fredo's.

"Fredo Rodriguez!" Señora Alonzo's eyes squinted into slits and her singsong voice turned low and rough, like she'd swallowed gravel. "That is an *Americano* song. Elvis *es un Americano,* and so am I."

In our house, *gringo* was a curse word. Papi would take the belt to me for sure if I ever used it. He said that Puerto Rico's people were all colors of the rainbow. So even if the green didn't like the yellow, one color couldn't disre⁄spect the other or pretty soon the whole rainbow would fall from the sky in broken colors. I assumed we were green and the *Americanos* were yellow.

But Fredo didn't stop there: "I'm not allowed to sing *Americano* songs, and anyone who sings those are *gringos* too." His voice was clear and defiant, but he looked down, his eyes drawing lines on the wooden desktop.

"You're allowed to speak *Inglés.* Why aren't you allowed to sing?" Señora Alonzo stood with her hands on her hips, her face flushed pink.

"Papá said," Fredo replied, his voice now quiet and small.

Señora Alonzo breathed loud. The air came out of her nose like wind and we were all silent, listening and hold⁄ing our own breaths.

"*Estudiantes,* take out your Dick and Jane books. *La música se termina.* Time for *Inglés* reading. Perhaps, Fredo, your papá will not object to you learning how to read Eng⁄lish."

I opened the top of my desk and hid behind the lid. "Fredo!" I hissed below the shuffle of books and papers and desk lids closing. "She'll tell your papá and he'll whip you for sure!"

"No, he won't. He says we should be more like Cuba. Besides, she's just a woman," he snapped back.

I gritted my teeth and squeezed the desk lid, flexing my muscles. "If you say that one more time, I'll punch you in the face!" I sliced my eyes the way Señora Alonzo did, took out my Dick and Jane, and slammed the lid closed. The sound was louder than expected. I jumped a little. So did Fredo, which was what I'd wanted in the first place.

Fredo was a runt. He always brought butter sandwiches fried in pork grease for lunch, making the whole classroom stink like dead pig. We nicknamed him *cerdito*, piglet, and called him that when he wasn't around. It didn't matter that he was Boricua or a boy—I was three inches taller, with muscles twice as thick.

I traced my fingers along the cover of *Streets and Roads*. Jane with her pretty blond hair tied in a bow. Dick in perfectly tucked shirt and shorts. Both were yellow-skinned and smiling. I liked the cover picture best. When I bruised myself from climbing the Flamboyán trees or tripping over dried sugarcane stalks, my skin turned yellow outside the round purpling. I figured it was the closest I could come to being like Jane. Jane on the cover, at least. Inside the book, her skin was as American white as the paper she walked on.

I was mad at Fredo for ruining our music class, for calling Elvis a *gringo*, for saying Señora Alonzo was just a woman, and, most of all, for reminding me that I was green and they—Elvis, Dick, Jane, and even Omar—were yellow. I was happy thinking of myself as a rainbow, like Papi said, until someone like him reminded me that I was greener than any other color.

" 'John and the Robbins,' " Señora Alonzo read aloud. Her voice was softer now. "Verdita, *por favor*."

I opened the worn cover and flipped to the chapter. Cars, tall buildings, and a bus with two layers were drawn across the top of the page. I put my finger to the first sentence, holding it down so my eyes could see.

"Park Street was a very busy street. In a very big city," I read aloud. Papi was a good reader and made me practice reading the newspapers that Tío Orlando sent from Washington, D.C. Omar sometimes brought comic books when he came. Archie was my favorite.

"Swish, swish went the a‑oo‑tu‑mo‑bb‑bb‑ay—" My face went hot.

"Auto‑mobeeles," Señora Alonzo sounded out.

"What's that?" I asked. I'd never heard the word before.

"*Un coche*. Like a car," she explained.

"Is an auto‑mo‑beeles different from a car?"

"No. But there are many words for the same thing in *Inglés*. We must learn them all."

I understood because even I had two names.


THAT EVENING, PAPI brought home a sack of yuccas. We sat on the veranda cutting the bark off. The rain clouds of the day had swept off to the west, streaking the horizon in silvery purple. The sun was out, melting pink and orange into the dark waterline. I watched the sky on fire, paying little attention to the root half-peeled in my palm.

"What's on your mind, Verdita?" Papi asked.

"Nothing," I said.

"Don't lie to your papi."

But I really wasn't lying. Other times I had said nothing, but I was thinking about the cockfight and Omar or the States and President Kennedy or the baby. Other times I had lied because I was thinking a lot of things. But now I truly wasn't. This time it was like I was melting into the sea foam with the sun. But I knew Papi wouldn't give up. So I asked, "Papi, do you like Elvis?"

"What?" With his knife still in hand, he scratched his forehead with his knuckles. The blade flashed speckles of gold.

"Fredo Rodriguez said that his papá hates *grin*—Elvis." I flicked the peels off my lap and reached for another root.

"Everyone is entitled to his opinion, Verdita. For me," Papi said, continuing to skin his yucca, "Elvis grunts too much. Reminds me of a pig taking a mud bath." He made *uh-huh* oinks and I laughed, thinking of Fredo and wishing someone would throw him in the dirt where he belonged. "Do *you* like Elvis? That's the better question."

"We sing his songs in music class."

Papi cocked his head and sucked his teeth.

"I like *Americano* music better than ours—better than

*jíbaro* songs." I couldn't look Papi in the eyes when I said it. If I did, I knew for sure I'd cry. I meant to show him that I had changed; we were different. I was more like Señora Alonzo than Mamá.

My blade caught on the bark. I tried to push it free, but it snapped the yucca in half and sent the narrow end skittering across the veranda. Papi watched until its spinning stopped, then took the peeled end from my hand. "I think we have enough." He put it into the pot and went inside.

*Chapter Four*

# A Taste of America

O
N THE MORNING OF DECEMBER FIFTEENTH, I
woke early to the smell of Papi's cologne on the
warm shower air. Old Spice. The only cologne
for island men, he said. It had ships on the bottle. Expen‑
sive. Papi only wore it on special days like today.

I kicked off the covers and followed the scent to his
room. Mamá was still in bed beneath a yellow crocheted
blanket. Waves of dark hair lay across the pillow, but her
face was hidden.

"Mamá," I whispered.

She didn't move.

"President Kennedy," I reminded her. It took her nearly
twice as long as Papi and me to get ready. If she didn't get
up soon, we'd be late.

The room filled up spicy. Papi said, "Mamá is sick,
Verdita."

He wore a powder-blue, pressed *guayabera* and had pomaded his hair up and back, slick and glossy. He looked like Elvis. No, Papi was more handsome.

"She has morning sickness," he said.

"Morning sick?" I'd never heard of such a thing.

"It's like catching the mountain mist," he explained.

It happened sometimes if you went out in the rain on the mountains of Puerto Rico. Salty ocean water came down in heat, then rose up again in cold mist. If you breathed in too much of it, the mist settled in your nose, your chest, your head, making you cold and achy. The day before when the rain fell, Papi and I had stayed inside and dry, but Mamá had gone to Señora Lopez's house, returning with damp hair and lungs.

Papi sat on the edge of the bed. "Leave Mamá to sleep. Go get ready."

I left their bedroom and dressed. Mamá was ruining our trip. I figured she'd done it on purpose, had gone out and breathed the mountain mist to keep me from doing what I wanted—seeing the United States. That was just like her. I pulled my hair back into one big ponytail and licked the flyaways to make them stay. I hated those black, corkscrew curls. A pair of round-tip scissors lay in a pile of crayons and colored pencils beside my dresser. I picked them up and snipped off a couple of curls near my temple.

Perfect. I was ready to meet the President.

I heard Mamá's and Papi's voices, whispering low, and I wondered what secrets they shared. I didn't like to leave them alone together for too long anymore, so I slid my feet into sandals and hurried back to their room. The whispers stopped as soon as I entered.

"Is she going?" I asked.

Papi patted Mamá's shoulder. "No."

She was a *jíbara* woman who never took an interest in anything away from our mountain *barrio*. I stamped my feet in the bedroom doorway. My sandals clattered on the tiles like flamenco shoes.

Papi stood and put his wallet in his pocket. *"Vámonos."*

When I realized we were going without her, electric pulses zipped through my legs. I shuffled down the hall making similar but very different clicks on the terra-cotta. Papi chose me over her, over Omar, over everything finally.

It was an hour to San Juan. We drove in Papi's jeep, top down, and I sat in the front since Mamá wasn't there. The sun shone; the rains had passed. The trees and grass were emerald bright and winking as we drove down our winding mountain. Fruit stands stood at every bend. Oranges, bananas, and pineapples. Along the straightaway, a man sold fried chicken from the back of his pickup truck with a fryer sticking out of the bed. We passed the *jíbaros* bar, the *Schitz* sign dark in the daylight. I thought of Omar for an instant. We drove on. A lone goat gnawed on the jungle brush where the mountain fell steep to a mossy waterfall. A pack of dogs ran beside us for a while, their black marble eyes never blinking. We passed another bar with *Navidad* lights strung across the front and three plastic kings, like stairs on the roof. Round and round, down we went until the jungle gave way to paved roads, a Walgreen's, concrete buildings, and a new Big Boy restaurant. Painted just above the doorway was an American boy in red checkered pants and slicked-back hair like Papi's. It had been a long time since I had been down the mountain. Not since we took Omar to the airport in August. The Big Boy hadn't been there then.

"Look, Papi," I pointed to the restaurant and read the sign. *"Hamburguesas."*

Papi gave a little snort and sucked his teeth.

"Can we try one on the way home? Real *hamburguesas Americanas?"* I had only ever seen hamburgers on the television commercials. I didn't know what they were, but the people in the commercials said they were delicious.

"Your mamá will have dinner waiting," he explained, but I saw him eyeballing the restaurant in his rearview mirror.

When we arrived in Old San Juan, some of the streets were blocked off for cars; crowds of tourists and islanders pushed their way along the cobblestones. Policemen with guns stood on the corners talking and adjusting the rifles slung across their backs. All my life I'd been around machetes and knives that were used for farmwork or protection, but never guns. They were only used for one thing, to kill. I rolled up my window a little and wished for a moment that I was home snuggled in bed with Mamá.

We drove on past the pink and orange buildings, past the Plaza de Colón with Columbus standing proud. If only he could see the island now—Indian and Spanish, American and African, green, blue, yellow, red—all blended together. We followed the road along the fortress wall, a thin brown line between the green lawn and the green sea.

"Mamá Juanita is meeting us in the Plaza San José," Papi explained. She'd just returned from visiting the United States.

We thanked the Virgin Mary hanging from the rearview mirror when we found a parking spot. A policeman with a rifle leaning on one shoulder stood in front of the Museo de San Juan, so I held Papi's hand while we walked. Across the boulevard, it seemed only the stone wall of El Morro kept the ocean from flowing into the city. I could almost touch it. From our porch, the water seemed so far. I wondered what Mamá would say if she was here, so close to the Ocean King again. I imagined him sending a giant wave over the city wall to sweep her back beneath. I shivered at the thought and was glad she was home safe.

We took a turn and followed the crowd that dipped down a narrow street. Vendors littered the sidewalk with carts of peeled oranges and *piraguas*. Tall buildings with carved archways and bright flags lined the cobblestone. Tourists with bulky cameras around their necks stopped and did backbends to take pictures of the old towers. A man in Bermuda shorts put his arm around the statue of

Ponce de León while his wife told him to say "cheez." Americans, the first white ones I'd seen up close. The woman's face was freckled pink, but her legs stuck out from under her skirt, thick sticks of bleached sugarcane. The man's head was bald and shiny red. I'd never seen such candy-cane people. Or maybe they painted themselves up that way for the *Navidad*. How strange they were. I wanted to take a closer look, but Papi pulled me away. In the middle, on a park bench, Mamá Juanita sat with a book under a plum umbrella. She wore a white cotton dress and shone as bright as the sun.

"Mamá!" Papi called.

She looked up and smiled, *"Ay Faro!"* She kissed Papi's cheeks. I hadn't seen her since the day before my birthday when she'd taxicabbed up the mountain with three dozen *besitos de coco* macaroons, only to realize it was the wrong day. But I didn't mind. It meant I got to celebrate for two days instead of one.

*"Bendición,"* I said.

*"Dios te bendiga en el nombre del espíritu santo."* God bless you in the name of the Holy Spirit. Mamá Juanita was a devout Catholic, even more than my mamá, which was hard to imagine. She kissed my cheeks twice over and crossed my forehead.

"You have grown so tall—and what a beauty. You have my eyelashes, you know." She batted them. They looked like two black flies caught on her face. I laughed. It felt nice to be beautiful like Mamá Juanita.

"And how is my prince?" she asked.

Papi was the eldest of Mamá Juanita's boys and the only one she called a prince. All of her children had moved to the States except Tío Benny and Papi. She flew to Washington, D.C., and Miami for holidays, but stayed mostly in San Juan. She liked it in the city. She'd never truly been a *jíbara* woman.

"I'm fine, but Venusa is sick," he replied.

Mamá Juanita opened her eyes big and stuck out her lips. "I hope it isn't the cancer."

My heart quickened. That's how Abuelo died. Cancer. He'd been overseeing the *finca* like any other day when he got a sudden pain in his middle. The doctors said the tumor had been growing in him for years. I looked to Papi and ground my back teeth against each other. I didn't want Mamá to die. I didn't hate her that much.

Papi shook his head. "Morning sickness."

"Ah." She smiled. "Tell her to have *sopa de leche* and a sip of *malta*—she'll be fine." She patted Papi's cheek.

I unclenched my jaw.

"Are you ready to see *el presidente de los Estados Unidos*?" she asked.

"*Sí.* President John F. Kennedy." Papi had taught me to say his full name perfectly.

"And so smart!" she said. Papi winked at me for doing well on the name, and I batted my eyes at him the way I'd seen Mamá Juanita do it. She took my hand in hers, soft from cocoa butter, like Mamá's. "*Vámonos*," she said, and we followed the crowds down San José Street toward the Plaza de Armas and City Hall.

The crowd filed into the square. A large woman who smelled of witch hazel and *café* stood in front of me. I tried not to breathe her in. Boys and girls my age and younger already claimed seats on top of the Four Seasons statues around the plaza. Papi tried to make room for us to squeeze closer to the front, but no one would budge.

"This is fine, Faro," Mamá Juanita said.

"Can you see, Verdita?" Papi asked.

I could see every stitch in the witch-hazel woman's teal *pantalones*, but that was about it. "No, Papi."

He tried to move me, but the crowd was thick. Someone gave a push, and I was sandwiched between the witch hazel and a man who spoke a language I had never heard before, neither Spanish nor English. It sounded like the last time I was sick and coughed up green chunks. I held my breath and tried to sing a song to myself—one of Mamá's nursery rhymes—but the heat of the day and the bodies around made it hard to keep a tune that didn't follow the pounding in my temples. And then something started to rise from my stomach, a hot taste, like an iron spoon left in the soup pot. The colors around me, the brightness of Mamá Juanita's dress, the blue of the *pantalones*, the green of the trees, all began to darken, to turn to grays. I looked up to the sky, trying to breathe, trying to reach the fresh air, but I couldn't swallow it fast enough. The darkness crawled over and everything faded. The smells and sounds turned to tastes: burning and bitter. The American and Puerto Rican flags flew side by side over City Hall. Red, white, and blue. Red and white. White.

I leaned forward and threw up. The crowd opened into a ring. Papi, Mamá Juanita, and I stood in the center of the *gallera*. All eyes on us.

*"Ay bendito!"* said the witch-hazel woman. Her face twisted, and she gagged.

Papi scooped me into his arms and carried me out of the plaza, my legs wrapped around his waist like when I was little. We walked away from City Hall, Governor Muñoz, and President John F. Kennedy.

*"Es* okay, *es* okay," Mamá Juanita kept saying.

I couldn't stop the tears from coming. It wasn't okay. I wanted to see America.

Papi walked us back to the long, green lawn in front of El Morro. He took off his *guayabera,* spread it over the grass, and I lay down. The wind swept over my body and I could breathe again. My tears dried in salty streaks. I was glad they were gone. I didn't know what had risen up or why, but I was mad at myself for it.

Mamá Juanita bought a tamarind *piragua* and sat beside me, pulled my head into her lap, into a sea of soft white. She opened her umbrella, stuck the handle into the ground, and fed me sweet ice in the shade. Papi lay in his undershirt, his hands beneath his head.

"I'm sorry," I said.

"Sorry? *Por qué?*" Mamá Juanita asked.

"We missed President Kennedy." I ran my hand over a patch of *morivivi*, life-and-death miracle plants. They pulled their fanned leaves into long prayerful limbs and *muerto*, died.

Papi stretched out long and crossed his ankles. "He is just a man, Verdita. You are my daughter. I can read about it tomorrow. Besides, your mamá is right. I don't trust these slick-tongued politicians. I'll wait to see what the newspaper says." He turned his face toward the sunshine. "It's good to be Boricua today, eh?" He nodded up.

A group of children flew kites. The wind blew steady and held the paper shapes high in the cloudless sky. The three of us lay on the lawn, watching them swoop and dart, swimming on the sea breeze. It was a beautiful day. I thought of Omar in the States. I doubted his sky was nearly as warm and clear. When I looked down again, the *morivivis* had opened back up, come back to *vivo*, life.

WE DROPPED MAMÁ Juanita at her pineapple-colored house near the University of Puerto Rico, so she wouldn't have to ride the bus.

"*Gracias*, Verdita," she said through the jeep window. "For what?" I asked.

"For the afternoon. I couldn't have prayed to spend it any different," she said, and kissed my forehead. "*Bendigo.*" Bless you.

At that moment I loved Mamá Juanita best of all. She

winked at me, hazel-gold flints in the sun. And when we drove away, I felt a pinch inside that made my eyes water and sting. I wished we lived in San Juan with her, not high up on the mountain, so far from the ocean and the rest of the world.

"Are you still feeling bad?" Papi asked.

I leaned my head into the crook of my arm, my elbow sticking out the car window. "No." I took a bite of the rushing air, eating the wind like it was the doughy middle of *pan de agua*.

"Hungry?" Papi asked.

I wasn't paying attention to the road ahead, focusing instead on grabbing the wind with my hand and pushing it into my mouth. We took a sharp turn, and my eyes snapped forward to the steady gaze of the American Big Boy.

"But Mamá?"

"We can eat her dinner for lunch tomorrow."

I imagined Mamá sitting at home alone over a bowl of *mixta*. She'd probably be happy eating nothing but rice and beans until the day she died. Not me. I kissed Papi's cheek as we pulled into the Big Boy parking lot. Inside, there was a short line leading up to the counter, where a large menu sign hung above a young man in a bright red and white uniform. Across the counter, fat bulbs of colored lights blinked steadily on and off. I couldn't help but stare. The colors felt good.

"You want a *hamburguesa*?" Papi asked.

But the menu wasn't just hamburgers. To the left was

the breakfast list: hotcakes, toast, sausage, and eggs. In the middle, chicken cooked five ways, soups, colossal onion rings, and the Big Boy double-decker hamburger. To the right, the desserts: strawberry pie, shakes, malts, *cafés*, and hot fudge sundaes. I was overwhelmed. I'd never been to a place with so many choices. Whatever Mamá made for dinner, we ate. And even the roadside kitchens only sold one thing at a time. Fried chicken or fish. Rice and beans. From the backs of trucks, farmers might sell a bunch of different fruits: oranges, bananas, mamey, custard apples, passionfruit, and acerolas. But I could get those from walking through our *finca*. I'd never been to a place with so much I hadn't tasted. One cook could not make this much every day. Maybe the food grew from magical American beans—fields of fried onions and hamburger buns.

We reached the front of the line and the man in red and white said, *"Feliz Navidad.* Welcome to de Beeg Boya. May I take jur oda?"

A *jíbaro*. He didn't speak proper English like we did.

*"Sí, una hamburguesa Americana,"* I said.

*"Y para usted?"* He looked at Papi.

Papi sucked his teeth. *"Una hamburguesa Americana también."*

We paid, and the man gave us a plastic card with a number. We took a seat in the dining room. At the head of our table was a cardboard flyer with a cartoon of Santa Claus in a checkered Big Boy shirt. He flew across a dark sky behind two lines of horses with tree branches coming out of their heads. In one hand he held a double-decker hamburger; in the other, the reins.

"Papi, why do they put sticks on the horses' heads?" I asked.

"Those aren't sticks, they're reindeer," he said.

"Why do they put reindeer on the horses' heads?"

Papi laughed. "No, Verdita. Those aren't horses. They're reindeer. They have horns like goats," he explained.

I'd never seen reindeer before, and Santa Claus had just started coming to Puerto Rico for the *Navidad*. Mamá and Papi said that he used to fly right over when they were young. It was a small island. And in the dark, back when not everybody had electricity, I could imagine we were easy to miss. Until this year, he had only visited the homes in the cities. Now he was coming to our mountain *barrio*. Papi saw the announcement in the newspaper and told me. I was sure it was going to be the most exciting *Navidad* ever. First, Saint Nicolas Claus would bring me presents and then, a week later, gifts from Saints Gaspar, Melchor, and Baltasar.

"There aren't any reindeer in Puerto Rico. Right, Papi?" I asked, still staring at the cartoon.

"*Sí.*"

"Are there reindeer in the States?"

"I think so."

"Does Omar have reindeer in Washington, D.C.?"

"Maybe."

We split a Coca-Cola, but I drank most of it before

the man brought our food. When he did, I had to turn the checkered paper tray around three times. It was the biggest sandwich I had ever seen, let alone eaten. I could tell that Papi was surprised too. He asked the server for a knife and fork, but the man said that most people used their hands.

"In the estates, they pick it up. *Como esto.*" The man cupped his hands into two Cs and pretended to take a bite.

"*Gracias,*" Papi said, and picked up the hamburger as the man had shown. I did the same.

"I guess you have to eat American hamburgers like an *Americano.*" Papi shrugged and bit into the sandwich. Some red sauce seeped out the side and landed in a glob on the table. He wiped it up with his napkin and chewed, his cheeks bulging.

I tried to get my mouth around mine, but could only manage to take a chunk out of the white bread. I tried again and hit meat. It didn't taste like I expected. Not like the men and women on television said it did. Sweet and spongy, it left my mouth feeling slimy around the corners.

"It's good?" I asked Papi.

He turned the hamburger around and set it back in the tray.

I tried to smile, but my lips slid apart on the sugary grease. The bottom one pouted out. "They're fun to eat," I said and C-cupped my hamburger again, this time nosing my mouth beneath the bread. I didn't want Papi to think I was ungrateful for my food. And if Americans liked hamburgers, then they had to be good. I figured I'd get used to the taste soon enough. "Do you think President Kennedy eats hamburgers?" I asked.

"Probably."

"Do you——" I started to say, chewing on a hunk of beef.

"Verdita, we may be eating American food, but we aren't American cowboys chewing tobacco. Swallow first. Then speak."

Papi chewed tobacco sometimes. I decided not to bring that up. Instead, I swallowed. "Do you think he likes them?"

"You should never presume to know a man's likes or dislikes——only your own."

Papi's hamburger sat on the tray. One bite in the side. I had a pretty good guess about Papi's dislikes, but I kept quiet.

I ate until my stomach pushed into the table ledge. I didn't even really like the hamburger, but I liked that it came from America——that I was eating like an American. It made me feel bigger than my *finca* on the mountain, bigger than the whole island. I'd seen the States, even if I hadn't seen President Kennedy. My stomach was full of America.

We took our leftovers home in brown bags. I still had half of my Big Boy double-decker. I'd save it, freeze it next to the plucked chickens and ripe bananas. Then later, when I wanted to eat America again, I'd have it ready.

"You weren't hungry?" I asked when we were back in the jeep, the Styrofoam box on my lap, Papi's whole hamburger alongside my half.

"Not too much. I need your mamá's food to fill me up."
He turned the ignition key, and we started our drive back
up the mountain. I'd freeze his too, just in case he changed
his mind. Just in case Mamá's food *wasn't* enough.

We didn't talk on the ride home. My stomach was too
full to feel, my mouth too slick for words. So I closed my
eyes and pretended that I was outside my body, flying
through the dark like the Big Boy Santa Claus, like President Kennedy in his airplane. Flying to the States.

*Chapter Five*

# A Taste of Puerto Rico

THE *NAVIDAD* FELL ON A MONDAY THAT YEAR. The Saturday before, there was a *parranda*, and our house was the start. Relatives began arriving in the afternoon. Tío Benny, Titi Ana, and my cousin Adel came extra early. They brought Tío's guitar and a pan of creamy *tembleque* for our feast, since their house was too far to be part of the progression. Titi Lola and Tío Chacho arrived soon after with my cousins Delia, Teline, and Pepito. Teline and I were the same age, but Delia was sixteen and already a *señorita*, so she didn't play with us as much as she used to.

"*Hola*, Verdita," Delia said, and kissed both my cheeks. She smelled strong. Like the incense they flung around during mass. I wondered if she had just come from confession and what she'd confessed. Mamá said once you became a *señorita*, everything changed. She said that Titi

Lola took Delia to confession twice a week so that the priest could make her right with God. I wondered if I would have to go that often when I became a *señorita*. I hoped not. I smelled like coconut bark, and I liked it that way.

Teline came in with Pepito. He was only three years old and still needed someone to watch after him. When Teline stopped to hug and kiss my cheeks, Pepito pulled away and ran toward the line of potted poinsettias that Mamá had bought for decoration.

"Pepito!" Titi Lola yelled, barely inside the doorframe. She'd dyed her hair purple-red and wore a grass-green dress that cinched at the waist then belled out to her knees. Her gold stiletto heels made little click-click noises wherever she walked.

Pepito ripped pointy leaves from their stems, but before he brought the red handfuls to his mouth, Titi Lola click-clicked to him and pulled him back by the forehead. "Teline, you almost let Pepito die!" She emptied his fists. Jagged petals confettied the floor.

"It's not my fault," Teline said.

"Your brother is little. You must watch over him," she scolded, then lifted Pepito onto the ledge of her hip and headed to the kitchen. "Mami is here." She kissed him, leaving a smear of fuchsia across his temple.

Teline got blamed for everything Pepito did wrong, because he was the only boy in the family. It wasn't fair. I did *not* want Mamá to have a boy. I took Teline's hand and led her away to the quiet corner of the living room where

Papi had put up a plastic tree with colored lights and a blinking star on top. I'd covered the limbs with silver tinsel like I'd seen in a magazine. The tree stood about my height, but if I lay down next to it, it seemed a hundred feet tall. I pulled her to the floor next to me; the crinoline beneath our skirts stuck up like white branches.

"Do you like our tree?" I asked.

"*Sí,* we have one too. Mami got it at Walgreen's," she said.

"My papi says Santa Claus is coming. Someone finally told him about our *barrio.*"

"Santa Claus? Delia says he's an old white man who only visits families on the mainland." She pulled a tinsel strand off a lower limb and wrapped it around her thumb.

"No, he's a saint—Santo Nicolas Claus. He comes to everyone in the world. My papi said so. It was in the newspaper," I corrected her. "Don't believe Delia. She's just mad 'cause she has to go to confession. Probably because she doesn't believe in saints!"

"No, Delia goes to confession because she has a boyfriend." Teline covered her mouth to keep in the laughs. But I didn't.

"A boyfriend!"

I knew that some *señoritas* had boyfriends that made them do crazy things, like scream and throw plates or dance in the rain. I'd seen it all on Mamá's *telenovelas*. She watched them in the afternoons while crocheting, pausing every so often from her counting to say *Ay bendito!* and cluck her tongue.

"Shhh," Teline warned. Delia stood a few feet away in the kitchen. Teline rolled over on her stomach. From where I lay, the layers of fluff haloed her head like an angel. She cupped her mouth and whispered, "Sometimes she goes in the back shed with him. I see them. Like when the rooster climbs on the hen. He rubs her and kisses her *tetas*. And she makes noises like this, oooo—ahh—*sí*—oh, *sí*."

I thought of Mamá and Papi on the couch, and the roosters I'd seen pecking hens, pecking each other—the blood of the *jíbaros* bar and the sound of bone against bone. I stopped laughing. Teline rolled around next to me in a fit of giggles.

"Not funny," I said, my face hot, my heart pounding.

Teline cocked her head. "Did you hear what I said?"

"*Sí.*" I pulled away.

"What's wrong, Verdita?"

"Who cares about Delia and her boyfriend." I got up. My red-striped dress was caught in the crinoline. I worked around myself, smoothing the stiff bristles. Teline stood and did the same.

"I'm sorry. Don't be mad." Her eyes were big as eggs.

I wasn't mad. I was something else. But I couldn't explain that to her. So instead I kissed her cheek. "It's okay."

"Girls," Titi Lola called. "Come help." We went to the kitchen. "See this." She held out a large bowl. "See those." She pointed to a basket of eggs. "Now, crack these eggs and put the yolks in the bowl. Just *yemas*. Don't get your dresses dirty." She tied a dish towel around my waist and did the same for Teline.

"What are we making?" I asked.

"Ahh!" She winked and smiled so that her eyes became slits. *"Co-qui-to."* She broke the word in three parts. "Some for tonight, some for *el Día de los Inocentes y los Días de Reyes* and the rest for in between. Go on, crack crack," she said and waved a hand.

We smashed the shells against the bowl's edge. It was fun to feel them break inside my palm. I ran my fingers over the smooth sides before crushing it into sharp pieces. My hands felt powerful.

The troubadours arrived just as Teline and I finished the last egg. Our fingers were sore from breaking the shells and scooping out the yellow. We only threw out three that bled orange red sunsets, silent baby chicks. The juice stuck to my palms. At the door, Papi greeted the men and welcomed in their bongos, *guiros,* guitars, and mara cas. The troubadours' songs were better than any other music—*jíbaro* or American—because they weren't just cho ruses and chants hummed over and over, they were sto ries, long and real and full of adventure.

Papi led the musicians through the kitchen back door to the outside tent he'd put up for the *parranda.* All of my cousins and Tío Benny filed out behind. I wanted to go too, but I couldn't leave Teline, and my hands stank raw. Mamá mixed the yolks with a wire whisk while Titi Lola added thick, sweet milk from a can, juice squeezed from the coconut flesh, sugar, and rum.

On the way out, a young troubadour with maracas nodded hello to Mamá and Titi Lola, then shook his batons. *"Me gusto coquito, coquito, coquito. Ay mi coquito, bebo todo el día,"* he sang, and shimmied to the door.

Mamá and Titi Lola laughed loud and hummed the tune as they mixed, their hips swaying.

"Taste," Mamá said. She poured the creamy mix into a chipped china cup and handed it to Titi Lola.

Titi drank and puckered her lips. "More rum."

They went on mixing and singing.

"Taste taste," Mamá said again, and she handed Titi the cup again.

"Almost," Titi Lola said, and poured in gulps from the gold-labeled bottle.

"Can I taste?" Teline asked.

"No, not until you are older. This is for the mamás and papás," Titi explained. "But you can dance with me."

She took Teline by the hands and twirled her around. *"Me gusto coquito, coquito, coquito . . ."*

Mamá put down her whisk and clapped along, salsaing to the rhythm. "Come on, Verdita," she called.

I had been mad at Mamá for months, but it was the *Navidad*, and Santa Claus was coming with reindeer, and we were having a *parranda* with troubadours, and despite myself, I couldn't help but miss her, just a little. So I figured, for that night I could forgive. I took her hand.

"Follow me," she said.

We danced around the kitchen, stepping back, stepping forward, spinning and moving our hips as we sang until Titi Lola's gold spike heel slipped beneath her and she nearly fell. Mamá caught her by the arm, and they laughed together until tears and spit mixed on their lips. Whatever this *coquito* was, it seemed to bewitch.

Titi took one last taste before deciding it was ready, and Mamá put a plate over the bowl. It had to marinate. Mamá and Titi Lola walked arm in arm to the *parranda* tent. More guests arrived, but, hearing the music, they followed the sound to the backyard instead of coming through the house. Teline and I were alone. Tío Benny's voice, already warm and sweaty with gin, began to sing. Mamá and Titi Lola's voices hummed along. I knew they were probably sitting under the tent, listening some, singing some, and all raising warm glasses. What magic this *coquito* must be for the troubadour to sing of it, for Titi Lola to say the word like a spell.

"Teline." I gestured with my lips toward the bowl. "Taste?"

"No! My mami will knot my head with *cocotazos*." She crossed her arms.

"I *dare* you to take one sip," I said. But Teline didn't know the States games.

"No," she said.

"Are you a chicken? Afraid?"

"*Sí*. Of my mami," she said.

I would never admit to a thing like that, and neither would Omar.

"Fine. I'll do it. I'm not a coward." I went to the bowl, making sure to check over my shoulder in case Mamá or Papi came inside.

I slid the lid halfway off. The smell burned my nose. *Medicina* and coconut soap. I wanted to cover it back up and forget the whole thing, but it was a dare—even if *I* had been the darer—and I couldn't let it beat me. Teline stood close behind, watching. I took up the big serving spoon that Mamá used for *mixtas* and dipped it into the cream. It was thicker than I'd anticipated, like rice soup or *tembleque* before it stiffened up. I looked back at the door. Mamá sang with Tío Benny, the troubadours played on.

"Quickly," Teline wheezed behind me.

I hesitated. Titi Lola had said that Teline couldn't have any. But I couldn't get in trouble, I reasoned, because Mamá never said I wasn't allowed. I lifted the spoon to my lips, holding my breath so my nose hairs wouldn't catch fire, and sipped. The smell didn't betray the taste. My throat burned, then cooled in a sweet candy coating. It was good. I put the whole spoonful in my mouth and gulped.

"What's it like, Verdita?" Teline pulled my arm.

"Ay! You'll make me spill." I licked the spoon clean and set it back on the countertop. "Coconut fire candy."

"I want to try."

I handed her the spoon. "You're still a scared chicken," I teased.

Teline ladled the mix into her mouth.

"*Ay bendito!*" She grabbed at her throat, her mouth turned down, and her nose flared. After a moment, she licked her lips. "It's not bad."

"*Sí,*" I said, and out popped a laugh. I covered my mouth and looked to the door. Still no Papi or Mamá. We took three more spoonfuls each; but then Tío Benny stopped singing, and I quickly licked the white off the back of the spoon and slid the plate over the bowl.

Papi came inside with Señor Lopez and some other *barrio* men.

"Don't you want to hear the troubadours, Verdita?" He palmed a couple of Schlitzes from the fridge and handed them around. The men popped open the tabs and sucked the fizz, their eyes glittering silver, their thumbs beating rhythms against the tin cans.

Papi went to the bowl of *coquito*. His hand was next to the serving spoon. He stood for a moment. I swallowed my heart and felt the thump-thump in the bony ridge of my throat. The heat of the *coquito* must have filled up my face. Sweat beaded above my lip and across my forehead.

He took off the plate, dipped his thumb in and sucked it.

"Venusa!" he called.

I closed my eyes. My eyeballs were hot under their lids. I had my defense ready: Titi Lola drank the *coquito*; Mamá never said I couldn't—

"*Coquito bueno!*" he said.

I popped open my eyes. Papi picked up an empty tumbler and scooped from the bowl. The coconut drink trickled down the sides. He licked the trails.

"Come on, Verdita. Teline." Papi ushered us through the kitchen door and out to the *parranda* tent. My legs felt heavy, my head light. Teline and I tried to share a plastic chair, but the puff of our skirts made us slide off. So we sat on the large wooden bench that stretched across the far end of the veranda. Our dresses fit perfectly on it, spread wide like peacocks' tails.

Teline giggled beside me. *"Me gusta coquito, coquito, coquito,"* she sang in a whisper, then broke into titters.

Nobody noticed Teline. She giggled all the time. It was when I started to do it that Mamá stuck out her lips from across the tent. She was watching me. The troubadours strummed their guitar and grated their *guiro*. They got the beat going before they picked a story. We all clapped along; my fingers tickled. I slapped them together and laughed.

"What kind of *bolero* should I sing?" the guitar-strumming troubadour asked.

"Sing about a woman," said Titi Lola.

"A beautiful woman!" someone shouted from the back of the tent.

"There once was a beautiful woman named Esmeralda," the troubadour began.

The rhythm continued, but he paused while a few others called out what Esmeralda's problem was. This was

how the troubadour ballads worked. The crowd called out
the hero or heroine and his or her problem, and the troubadour sang the story. Sometimes the crowd would only
give a word, a color, a place, and from that he spun a great
tale.

"She loses all her teeth," Señor Lopez laughed.

"She's a famous dancer," said Adel.

"She kisses boys in the shed!" Teline called out.

"Teline!" I covered my mouth for hers.

The troubadour continued singing. Nobody else heard
or noticed, but Delia did. She locked eyes with me, so dark
and shiny that I had to look away. The troubadour sang of
a beautiful woman who loved to dance, but fell in love
with a one-legged man who could not. And so, all her life,
she danced alone with only dreams of being in his arms.
It was a funny but sad song.

They continued to sing while we ate *pasteles* and roasted
pork. Mamá and Titi Lola brought out the *coquito* in an
old wine bottle. Mamá sipped on passionfruit juice, but
the rest of the mamás and papás passed around the bottle
until it was empty and their eyes sparkled in the moon-
light. Then the head troubadour announced it was time
to move on to the next house in the *parranda*, so we helped
Mamá put away the food in the kitchen before setting
down the gravel road to the beat of a bongo drum.

The next stop was the Santiagos'. Their house was on
a flat cliff near the edge of the road. From the yard, you
could see all the lighted houses on the side of the mountain

and into the dark valley below. The colorful *Navidad* strands and trios of glowing plastic kings made the mountain look bejeweled.

We sang at the Santiagos' front door until they came out, pretending to be surprised, and led us inside where plates of *arroz con dulce* and fried plantains waited along with more guests joining the progression. There I noticed a face I hadn't seen before, and there weren't too many I didn't know in our *barrio*. Usually, new faces came with births and old faces left in funerals. But this one was different.

"Who's that?" I asked Teline.

She giggled spit everywhere. "That's him!" she said. "Delia's boyfriend, Carlos. He came from San Juan. Got a job on the Santiagos' *finca*."

He was nice looking. Older than us. Older than Delia, but nowhere near Papi's age. His skin was dark and smooth, and he had no hair on his arms. His eyes were blue-purple; they seemed to change with the blinking strands of lights. I followed them, fixed on Delia. She sat on the other side of the room, drinking a can of guava juice and talking to the maraca troubadour. Flirting. I could tell by the way she played her fingers over the bones below her neck; the way he leaned in, forehead first, to hear her speak. The men and women on the *telenovelas* did it all the time. Their movements were slow and heavy, like strands of seaweed flowing in invisible currents. Carlos watched. Delia seemed not to notice.

"Mami calls him *Pasita* because of his hair," Teline laughed. "He runs errands for us at the salon when he's not busy at the Santiagos'. If Papá knew about Delia and him," she shook her head, but kept a smile, "he'd kill him."

The lead troubadour strummed his guitar and, one by one, the other instruments joined in. The maraca man left Delia, giving her a nod and a wink and a shake-shake of his batons. The music began, and it felt like I'd left my body, my spirit hovering somewhere between the notes and the voices, the vibrations and the colors, tasting only spicy coconut, even though I'd since eaten rice and *pasteles*. Delia stood and went toward the kitchen. The troubadour's high voice cried out. Another song was beginning, another story to tell.

"Verdita." Teline pulled hard on my arm. "Come!"

I followed her unsteadily, my legs wobbling beneath my candy-cane skirt.

"Where are we going?" I asked.

We flew through the kitchen, where the heat of the stove and the bodies made the air sticky, hot, and suffocating. Teline pulled me onto the veranda overlooking the jewel-sprinkled mountain, where it was cool and easy to breathe. Outside, the troubadours' song was no more than a hummed lullaby, a tiny rhythm against the *co-qui-co-qui* of the frogs and the ocean breeze rushing through palm fingers.

"Quiet. This way," she whispered. I followed her around

the side of the house where an old mango tree stood, its branches low and wide.

There was a hum, a whimper, then a scrape scrape. We tiptoed under the branches until we saw: Delia against the tree's trunk, her legs, long and shiny, around an invisible waist; her head separate from her body, thrown back and swallowed by darkness. She moved up and down, floating on the sea air. She was beautiful.

"See!" hissed Teline.

"How is she doing that?"

"Carlos," said Teline.

Suddenly, Carlos's form cut out of the black. The mountain lights reflected on his slick skin. Delia was not floating but pushed up by him. He pulled her forward. Her lips disappeared into his blackness and she moaned low and long.

"Is he hurting her?" I asked.

She shook her head. "She likes it. It feels good. Like this." She leaned in to my neck, pressing her lips, sucking and then releasing. Goosebumps spread over my arms and legs, and I knew what Mamá and Papi felt when they lay together on the couch.

"What else happens?" I asked.

"*Nada*. He puts *it* inside her and they sit like that, kiss, ing, until they stop." She shrugged her shoulders.

"Like the chickens," I said.

Teline nodded. "I heard Mami tell Delia that if she

doesn't watch out, God will punish her with baby chicks clucking at her heels."

"No." I imagined Delia laying an egg a day until Teline's house was full of little Pepitos. What a nightmare! Then I remembered Mamá and Papi. My throat closed up and burned hot coals. Was the baby their punishment? I crossed myself.

"Come on." Teline turned back to the house.

I started to follow, but in the dark, I couldn't see the thick roots of the mango tree sticking out like giant shoelaces. I tripped and fell forward in the dirt. The root twisted my ankle. I yelped before I could stop myself. I tried to get up, but my ankle was pinched sideways.

"Shhh!" Teline crouched low, hiding beside me.

"Who's there?" said Carlos. He walked toward us.

The dirt against my face smelled like avocado skin. Carlos's footsteps crunched the fallen mango leaves.

"Run!" Teline yelled, but Delia caught her by the arm. Carlos pulled me up and squeezed my shoulders until I was sure they bruised. Teline squirmed and twisted against Delia but couldn't get free.

"What did you see?" Delia asked. Her voice was clipped.

"I'll tell Papá if you don't let us go," said Teline. She kicked at Delia's shins.

"You little brat!" Delia slapped her cheek. Teline stopped struggling and began to cry.

"You tell anyone," Carlos looked at me, his eyes like black holes, "I swear I'll get you when everyone is asleep. They'll think the Chupacabra ate you up."

My knees shook. The air stopped moving. I couldn't even blink.

Delia pulled Teline close and sniffed her mouth. "You stink of rum. Don't think I don't know. You tell Papá, and I'll tell him you and little Verdi got drunk on *coquito*."

"We only had a few sips." Teline's mouth bubbled through the tears.

"We won't tell," I said.

"She's the smart one," said Carlos. He squeezed my shoulders again, and I bit my lip to hold back the sob.

"Wipe your face before you go." Delia let loose. Teline rubbed her arm over her eyes then ran fast, leaving me.

"Smart girl, you remember what I said," Carlos whispered into my ear. "Or it won't be Santa Claus visiting. It'll be the Chupacabra."

As soon as I felt the pressure release, I followed Teline in a sprint. Inside, the troubadours once again packed their instruments. The *parranda* moved on. I tried my best to brush the dirt stain from the front of my dress. Teline was lost somewhere in the crowd, hidden by song and story and *Navidad* feasting.

"Your dress." Mamá appeared behind me. She eyed the mud tracks.

I gulped, happy to see her and afraid she knew all I'd seen. "I fell outside on the mango roots," I said.

Mamá nodded. "Palmolive soap. Those stains will come out."

But Palmolive soap couldn't wash everything out, like I wished it could.

I wouldn't tell anyone about Delia and Carlos, not because they made me swear, but because I'd never be able to put into words what I'd seen.

THE FOLLOWING NIGHT it rained again.

"How is Santa going to see our *barrio*?" I asked Papi on our way home from *Nochebuena* mass.

"He will."

"But won't he get wet?" All the pictures showed Santa in a topless sleigh.

"So, he'll be a wet Santa," said Papi. We rode in silence the rest of the way.

That night, I couldn't sleep. I listened to every creaky palm tree and every lizard slithering through the window slats. I'd seen enough on television to know that bells would be the tip-off when Santa came. I wasn't listening for him, though, but Carlos. I kept my promise not to tell anyone, but what if Teline hadn't? She never could keep a secret. And she hadn't sworn under the mango tree, like I had. So I listened for footsteps, for whispers, for moans that came in the darkness.

I wasn't excited for the *Navidad*, like I thought I'd be. Instead, I worried that Carlos would come. That Santa wouldn't. My mind talked on and on, even when I was too tired to listen anymore. I rolled beneath the bedsheets, the wet heat sticking them to my legs. I sang *aguinaldos* from mass. I listened to the rain fall and prayed for it to stop before Santa came, then prayed for it to keep on to protect me from Carlos.

I woke to the sound of cocks crowing. The storm had passed. It was the *Navidad,* and I hadn't heard bells or footsteps. I got up, woozy from sleep and tired from not enough.

Outside in the living room, Papi sat on the couch, reading the morning paper. Mamá crocheted white and blue balls of yarn in her lap.

"*Feliz Navidad,*" she said.

Papi put down the newspaper and stuck out his lips toward the tree. "Looks like Santa made it through the rain."

*Turrón* candies were knotted to the plastic branches of the tree; beneath sat two boxes wrapped in brown paper and tied with red bows. It wasn't like I expected. Not like the television programs or the pictures of gifts Santa gave the children in the States. To their living rooms he brought live, giant trees strung with lights and popcorn and tinsel, and stuffed endless amounts of shiny presents beneath. I had two brown paper boxes and nougat candy tied with yarn that matched Mamá's crocheting.

"Go on. Open them," Mamá said, putting her needle down and kneeling beside me.

I pulled a box into my lap. Papi folded his newspaper and held it under his arm.

"Didn't Santa bring *you* presents?" I asked.

"He only brings children presents. You know that," said Papi.

I did know that, but I wondered if Santa would make up for the time he lost skipping over the island when they were kids. I always figured when he found our *barrio*, there'd be a ton of gifts for me and Papi and Mamá—gifts from all the *Navidades* before. Or at least one for each of *mine* he'd missed. I didn't want to seem ungrateful, but two?

I undid the bow of the first box and pulled the paper off in strips. It looked like the same brown paper we wrapped the raw fish and chicken thighs in. Underneath was a shoebox, and inside, a pair of white sandals with one-inch heels. My first pair of pumps. Santa *had* to be real—Mamá and Papi had said I couldn't have pumps until I turned a *señorita*. He'd be the only one to give me what I wished for.

Each shoe was stuffed with paper that smelled like the glue we used in art class at school. After pulling it out so I could try them on, the whole house smelled sour. I slipped my feet into the pumps and instantly felt older. The room shrank a little—Mamá and Papi too. I remembered how Titi Lola had shuffled through our kitchen just two days before, and I tried to imitate her walk, swaying my hips and taking little click-click steps.

"Aren't those nice." Mamá didn't say it like she was

surprised or angry that Santa disobeyed her. "And so white. You can wear them to church and they match all your dresses."

I squatted and slid my fingers over the slick patent leather. The only thing that perplexed me was the color. I asked Santa for *red* pumps. Either way, I was glad to have them, but obviously something in Santa's workshop was misunderstood. I picked up the shoebox. Across the lid were the words MONTGOMERY WARD. Santa got his gifts at Montgomery Ward? The television showed short men with pointy ears making toys at the North Pole. Before I had a chance to think, Papi handed me the second gift. I tore off the paper. It was a journal with gardenias drawn on a green, swirled background. The cover read *Diario de Meditación* in a loopy-loop script. It was beautiful. The cover creaked a little when I opened it; the pages were whiter than our Dick and Jane's, the edges as sharp as a knife. In the middle of the first page was an inscription: *Le pertenece a* and then a space. In it, *Maria Flores Ortiz-Santiago* was written in a handwriting I had seen before— Papi's.

In that moment, I saw it all. Mamá's yarn holding the *turrones* on the tree, our brown paper from the kitchen, the heels from the Montgomery Ward catalog, the journal that Papi had scripted my official name in. Papi and Mamá gave me these gifts, not Santa. There really was no Santa.

Tears welled. The colored lights on the tree spread out like globs of syrup in a *piragua*.

"Now you have a place to write," said Papi. "Good, clean pages." He took the journal and ran his hand along the spine.

I wished I could go back to the hour before, the day before, or even the year before, when there might be a Santa who just couldn't find our *barrio*, couldn't find Puerto Rico; back to before I saw Mamá and Papi on the couch, before the cockfight and Papi at the *jíbaros* bar. I wanted to forget everything and go to the States.

"*Feliz Navidad*, Verdita," Mamá kissed my head. "Do you want some mango for breakfast?"

I wasn't hungry, but I pulled an almond nougat off the tree and stuffed it in my mouth.

"You'll get sick if you eat candy so early," she warned.

I pulled another off. "I like it." I could lie too.

"No sweets this early," Papi said. We eyed each other without blinking, then the telephone rang. It was Tío Orlando in Washington, D.C., calling to wish us a Merry Christmas.

While Mamá and Papi handed the phone back and forth, I took my journal to my room and sat on the bed. With my pumps on, my feet could reach the floor; they couldn't when I was barefoot. I took a black pen and scribbled across where Papi had written my name. Over the black jungle of spirals and lines, I wrote *Verdita* in strong, straight print.

"Verdita!" Papi called from the living room. "Come talk to Omar."

I came out, still wearing my pumps, and click-clicked to the phone.

"You'll get holes in the soles before you've even worn them out of the house," Mamá said from the kitchen. She sliced a ripe mango, the mango I'd already decided I wasn't going to eat, no matter how much my stomach growled.

"Hello?" I said into the receiver.

"What's up?" said Omar.

"Huh?" I wondered how he knew I was wearing heels.

"Merry Christmas."

"Merr—" It was hard to say it like he did. My *r*'s kept rolling together. *"Feliz Navidad,"* I said instead.

"Santa finally make it to the *barrio* this year?" Omar asked. He didn't wait for me to answer. "I got a bike. You should see. It's practically brand new. My best friend, Blake—his dad's going to oil the chain for me."

"Blake? Who's that?" I asked.

"He moved in on my street. He's over right now 'cause I got this new board game called Risk. It's cool, man."

I didn't know why Omar was calling me a man, nor did I think playing a game where you were cold sounded like fun. Omar and his dumb games.

"Well, it's nice here. Not cold at all," I said. "I'll get my *real* gifts on Three Kings Day. I got new pumps—those are shoes with heels. And a journal."

"Cool," said Omar.

"No." I was confused and annoyed with Omar and his new best friend. "It's *warm*."

"Yeah, okay. Well, I got to go. Blake's ready to play. 'Bye, Verdita."

I handed the phone back to Papi.

"How's Omar?" he asked.

"Don't know. He had a friend over. They're playing some cold game." I rolled my eyes.

Truth was, I missed him. We never said we were best friends, but I always kind of thought it. It stung my ears to hear him say it about somebody else.

"Omar is stupid," I whispered under my breath. Papi heard.

He took the phone and scrunched his eyebrows together, but didn't say anything, just went over to Mamá and kissed her neck and took a bite of mango. I thought of Teline's kiss at the *parranda*; goosebumps rashed over my skin, and I shivered in the heat of Christmas morning.

## Chapter Six

# A Blond Bomb

B Y SPRING, THE CURLS I'D CUT AWAY ON THE DAY
we went to see President Kennedy had grown back
in sprouts that stuck straight out of my temples,
too short to pull back in my ponytail and too long to stay
hidden. I tried to pomade them down, but they always
sprang up and dried, crispy wet. Mamá noticed and asked
me what I'd done to myself. I told her it was *my* hair, and
I liked it that way, even though I didn't.

She started snooping through my stuff around then,
cleaning my room when I told her not to, asking if I had
any dirty clothes to wash, standing outside the bathroom
every time I came out. The two of us were home alone a
lot. Papi stayed out later and later. He said they were a man
short on the *finca*, but his razor box was empty. I knew
where he was. I hadn't forgotten the *jíbaros* bar—the piles

of money and the easy way he held the red playing cards. But I wouldn't tell Mamá. I'd keep his secret.

After school each day, I wrote in my journal on the front porch, making myself too busy to be bothered. I cut out pictures from Mamá's magazines and catalogs— pictures of pretty dresses and shoes and hairstyles. I taped them to the pages of my journal and wrote on the top of each why I liked them and where I imagined wearing the outfit. The first picture was the blond Simplicity girl with the bluebonnet dress. I liked everything about her: her dress, her shoes, her hair. At the top of the page, I wrote that I'd wear *her* every day and everywhere. I hid the journal under my mattress, pushing the book as far into the middle as my arm could reach. I didn't want Mamá finding it and reading, like I knew she would. It was only fair—if Mamá and Papi had secrets, I could have them too.

Around the same time, thin, light hairs grew down low on my private parts. At first it was just a few, and I pulled them out thinking that maybe the curlicues I chopped off my head had accidentally found a spot somewhere else. But where I plucked one, five more grew. I hadn't seen Mamá under her skirt before, but Papi's arms and legs had dark curls, so I figured I took after him. The coloring was different, though, and I liked it—light brown and sometimes blond in the light. Once a week I locked myself in my bedroom and used Mamá's clamshell mirror to look at them. I thought they were the prettiest part of me. I wanted all my hair to change color to match and thought maybe it would, but after a few weeks of waiting, the hair on my head stayed black and fuzzy. I was sick of looking at it, especially now, with the sprouts at my temples. Titi Lola owned a hair salon. If anybody could help, she could.

"I want to get my hair done," I announced one day. It was the first time I'd spoken directly to Mamá in a while. She smiled wide and put down the blue and white striped blanket she'd been crocheting since the *Navidad*. It lay over her lap like a giant doll skirt. "I want to go to Titi Lola's," I continued.

She eyed the frizz clipped sideways down my back. "I can call her today. I have to go to town on Saturday for an ALA meeting. I'll drop you at Titi's and run my errands, *sí*?"

That worked perfect, and it meant that Mamá wouldn't be hanging around the salon telling me how to do my hair. A few weeks before, she'd started taking English lessons through the American Legion Auxiliary, and I guessed they were working because she brought home a thick English textbook with more words than my Dick and Jane. She sat at the kitchen table reading for hours when she wasn't on the couch crocheting and watching *telenovelas*. It made me boiling mad. She was only learning English so Papi and I wouldn't have our own language anymore. She wanted to get between us and was using words to do it.

Titi Ana took Mamá to the ALA meetings. It was a women's club for the wives of the Borinqueneers. Papi was a Borinqueneer before I was born, and so was Tío Benny. They were part of the Sixty-fifth Infantry in Korea. Papi was in G Company. G like a *guiro*. Tío Benny was in C Company. C like a *cuatro* guitar. I imagined the Sixty-fifth as a big troubadour band, each company a different instrument. I liked thinking of Papi making the rat-ti-tat sound of a scraped hollow gourd while Tío Benny played his guitar. Papi didn't talk much about Korea except to say that the weather was bad and the food made him sick. He kept his uniform in the back of his closet. I used to sneak into his room and smell it. Korea was sweet and sour like *morcilla*, blood sausage. I licked it once to see if it tasted the same, but I only got a tongue full of fuzz that tasted like the bitter bark of sugarcane.

That next Saturday, after breakfast, Mamá came into my room. "Are you ready?" She wore a pink blouse that Vee-ed tight to her chest, then billowed out at the bottom where her waist was growing. I liked it, but I wouldn't tell her that. A red, white, and blue ALA badge with Papi's name and company was pinned to the left side of her shirt, just above the bulge of her breast.

"*Sí,*" I said, and slipped into my pumps. I was only a little shorter than Mamá in them. We almost stood eye to eye. I'd grown three inches since the summer before, and with the heels on, everything looked different. From there, I realized how small Mamá was: short, thin from her head to her waist, then plump from the hips down, like all the muscle and fat had run away from her head and settled in her *culito*. I was sure I took after Papi—tall, with long legs and strong arms. Papi and I could climb every tree on our *finca* while Mamá seemed to grow tired from lifting her crocheting needle. I couldn't wait until I was taller. That would be a fine day.

We normally walked to town, but Mamá had been sick on and off all winter. Now that she felt better, she didn't want to risk getting wet in a rain shower. Sometimes in the spring, showers passed from one end of the island to the other in a comb of water. Drenching rain for a minute, then mist rising before the sunshine. Since Papi was home putting up new wire fencing in the chicken coop and tending to the *gandul* bush in the garden—the green pigeon peas had mites—we took his jeep to town. Mamá kept the top up and barely let me roll down the windows; she said she didn't want the wind to mess her hair. Inside was hot and thick with her perfume; the bottled roses stank too candy-sweet to be natural. She kept the radio off and pumped the brake at every turn, starting and stopping all along the bendy road. It made my stomach feel like a beaten egg, frothy around the edges. I closed my eyes and hung my fingertips out the cracked window so they could drink in the air.

It took us twice as long to get to town as it did when Papi drove. When we finally pulled up to Titi Lola's salon, I opened the jeep door before Mamá put the car in park.

"*Ay bendito*, Verdita! You're going to kill yourself," Mamá said when I jumped out, the tires rolling to a stop. But I planned to be around long after her and then some.

Titi Lola's house had two levels. On the bottom was

the salon, with pink cushioned high chairs and long mir-rors strung around the room. On the top was their home: a small kitchen, a living room, Tío and Titi's bedroom, Delia's bedroom, and Teline and Pepito's bedroom. Delia and Teline used to share a room, but Titi Lola made Teline move in with Pepito once Delia became a *señorita*. I felt bad for Teline, having to live with a baby who still wet the bed, and a boy on top of that. I didn't have to share a room with anybody, and I never wanted to. The new baby could sleep in the tub for all I cared. My room was off limits.

I pushed open the door and stepped into the loud rhythm of a *bomba* coming from the old radio in the cor-ner; women chattered back and forth through the mirrors and across the room to each other; a hair dryer began to blow, and water ran in the sink. The salon always felt alive with change and newness. It was full of women, a few ac-tually getting their hair done while the rest sat in the high chairs reading magazines, tapping their feet to the radio, and lending an occasional *Ay, Dios mio!* to the gossip. Titi Lola stood in the middle with a paintbrush in one hand and a bowl of white paste in the other. An old, yellow-skinned woman with bits of hair poking through a rubber cap raised an eyebrow when I entered. She looked like a sea turtle, her skinny neck poking out of the green smock.

"Verdita! Here you are!" said Titi Lola. "You're right on time. Is your mamá with you?"

The last time I'd seen Titi Lola was at the *Navidad*. Her hair was red then. Now it was brown. I liked it better red.

*"Sí."* I nodded toward the door. The bell over it clanged when she entered. I hadn't heard it do that when I came in.

"Venusa!" everyone said at the same time.

Mamá moved around the room kiss-kissing cheeks. I followed behind, getting residual pecks before making my way to an empty high chair.

"I can't stay. I have an ALA meeting and then an appointment." Mamá stuck out her chest so everybody could see the pin.

"Oh, *sí,*" the turtle-lady said under her breath, obviously impressed that Papi was a Borinqueneer.

*"Bueno,"* Titi Lola said, and continued to paint.

"Okay. And Lola, do something with that hair." Mamá sighed. "I've tried everything."

I rolled my eyes. I did my own hair. Mamá hardly touched it except on special days. She made it sound like my hair was on *her* head. I'd show her. The Simplicity picture was in the pocket of my jean shorts. I could feel the paper stiff against my leg.

*"Adios!"* She waved to the room, then locked eyes with me. "Verdita, be good for Titi." She talked to me like I was still a *bebita.* I looked away and nodded. When she went out, the doorbell clanked again.

"I love this song," Titi Lola said, and a woman with hair knotted in rags turned up the radio. A *charanga* orchestra played out a fast rhythm. Titi Lola shook her hips and took quick back-and-forth steps around the turtle-lady.

"Cha-cha-cha, cha-cha-cha," she sang, then put the bowl and brush down.

"Verdita, what you want? Shorter? Bangs?" She fingered my sprouts.

I reached into my pocket and slid out the paper folded neatly in fourths. Titi Lola unfolded it and squinted.

"I want that," I said.

She lifted an eyebrow, and for a second I thought she'd say no.

"I was going to try blond next too." She laughed. "Do you like the brown?" She fluffed her hair and lifted her shoulder to her chin like the actresses in magazines.

"It's nice," I lied. I had to. I wanted her to make my hair blond and straight. I'd have said anything to get it done.

"Me too." She grabbed a green smock and spread it around my neck like a backwards cape. It was the first time I had my hair done at Titi's salon, and I seemed to fit eas-ily into the pink picture of the room in the mirror.

"You want it cut, too?" Titi Lola asked.

"I want it just like hers." I pointed again to the picture. "Straight and blond to my shoulders."

"Your mamá say okay?"

Mamá hadn't bothered to ask me anything about my hair. "She doesn't care."

"Okay." Titi Lola yanked out my elastic band, along with a few corkscrewed strands. "I think you'll look very beautiful with this blond hair. Oh, *sí.* I think so."

My chest zippered from my navel to my neck. This was it! I was going to be beautiful like the girls in the States—more beautiful than Mamá. Titi Lola brushed out the snarls, and my hair expanded, rising like a black sea sponge. I hated that reflection. Ugly and dark with island hair and island dirt. I was glad that when the day was done, it would be gone.

She trimmed my ends, then told me to lie back in the sink and squeeze my eyes shut. She applied a thick cream. It burned my forehead, the tips of my ears, and the back of my neck; even the hairs in my nose hurt from the smell. She combed; my scalp stung and itched, but Titi Lola assured me that it was a natural part of the process. She had to brush out the curls, had to show my hair how to behave, punish it for being unruly and disobedient. It was bound to hurt a little, like when Papi punished me. So I held my breath and dug my nails into the chair cushion until she finished and rinsed the fire from my head.

Water dribbled down my temples; my nose itched with no relief. Torture. Titi Lola cut squares of tinfoil from a long roll, poured a couple different bottles into a bowl, and mixed it with a paintbrush.

"Here we go. Magic time," she said and began painting and wrapping my hair in tin shingles until I looked like a cartoon spaceman on television.

I had to sit and wait for my hair to take the paint and change color. Titi Lola gave me a stack of magazines. I flipped through all the Spanish ones until I found an

English headline. A *TV Star Parade* with Cynthia Pepper on the cover saying, "The biggest fights with my parents ever." I liked her. Cynthia was blond, like I'd be; she had bangs that curled open like a flower, with the rest of her hair in two braids on each shoulder. I decided I'd wear my hair just like that tomorrow, and I wanted to rip out the photo for my journal. I paged through the advertisements until I found the section with her interview. I liked the American magazines best. They were easy to read and never had big words—like *automobile*.

I'd finished the Cynthia interview and an article on Elvis when Titi Lola tapped the tinfoil on my head with a comb. It sounded like dried banana leaves in the breeze.

"You ready to see your new hair?"

I'd been ready a long time. I leaned back in the sink. Titi Lola stripped off the tinfoil and poured warm water over. The smell was strong, like she was washing my hair in *coquito*. She hummed a little to the radio. It had been on the whole time, but I hadn't heard the songs. The music blended into the hum of blow dryers, the crackle of foil, the splashes of water, the talk of women.

"La·la da·da! You wanted blond hair—you got it," she said. "What they call them in the States? Blond·ay bomb·shell? You a blond·ay bombshell." She smacked her thigh with a wet hand before squirting shampoo into it and sudsing my head in gardenia·scented shampoo.

She scrubbed hard; it felt good after all the itchy creams from earlier. The muscles in her arms moved up and down under her skin. When she leaned in close to rinse my hair, her crucifix necklace spindled on my nose. Down her shirt, two large breasts hugged together in a black lace brassiere. Mamá had nice breasts too. Once, when she was dressing, I saw them, round and full, with two brown tips like passionfruit stems. While Titi Lola hummed and rinsed, I slid my hand up to my own chest beneath the smock, beneath the cotton of my shirt, and ran my fingers over *my* nipples. Goosebumps dominoed across my skin. The softness grew hard, and I noticed a lump beneath each tip. Breasts! I hadn't noticed the guava berries before. I ran my hand across again, proud of them, and at the same time ashamed that I was becoming more like Mamá.

*"Hola!"* Mamá suddenly appeared. I jerked my hand from my shirt, even though it was hidden, and eyed the wall clock. I'd been in the salon two and a half hours. She was already finished with her meeting. Lying back in the sink, I felt like she was standing on top of me, like I was a baby again looking way up to see her. I didn't like it.

"Venusa, you're just in time to see." Titi Lola helped me sit tall, and I felt more myself. A pale foreign wave fell across my eyes, and I pinched it to get a good look. It wasn't just blond. It was nearly white. I couldn't believe it was attached to my head. I pulled, truly believing that it might somehow unravel, like a piece of yarn.

*"Ay, Dios mio!* Lola, what have you done to her?" Mamá snatched at her chest.

"What do you mean? She wanted the blond and straight. She say you okay with it."

Mamá narrowed her eyes at me. "Your papi will be so angry!"

Titi Lola wrapped my hair in a towel and led me to the high chair. "You wait until it's done. It's not done yet. I fix, Venusa. No worry. I fix."

I sat down before the mirror. She pulled the towel off. White-blond waves fell to my shoulders. My skin seemed browner than it had before, my bushy black eyebrows like caterpillars across my forehead. Sweat beaded on my upper lip and forehead. I looked nothing like the Simplic-ity picture—nothing like Cynthia Pepper. I was a mon-ster! A Chupacabra! The same dirty island girl I'd been two hours ago, only now white-haired, like an old ghost.

I stared at the ceiling, at the floor, at Mamá pacing back and forth, at anything but my reflection; and I prayed that Titi Lola would make me beautiful like she promised. She set my hair in can-size rollers, tight pins jabbed my scalp, then put me under the dryer. It blasted hot air into my ears, softening the wax and making me deaf. I counted the lines on my palms until the process was com-plete, refusing to look up. Titi Lola had one last chance to change me into what I wanted. She used raspberry po-made to smooth the choppy locks around my face, to pull them straight. Out of the corner of my eye, I could see the greasy wings, slick and stiff.

"Okay," said Titi Lola. She spun me around to my reflection.

I was the ugliest girl I had ever seen. I ran a hand over the top of my head. The hair was coarse, like a horse's tail, despite the oily pomade. It wasn't straight or curly, but some unnatural in-between, like the coated feathers of the dead roosters in Papi's study. Nobody in Puerto Rico or the States would think I was beautiful.

"Your hair is very curly, Verdita. Very hard to make straight. I tried, but sometimes the cream don't work so good. But it is the color you wanted," she explained.

I wanted my old hair back. But I couldn't go back.

Mamá rubbed her eyes and crossed herself. "*You* will explain this to your papi, and *no* crying. You did this, Verdita." She shook her head.

"I'm not crying." The words popped out in a half-sob. "My head hurts. That's all." I prayed Mamá's hair would turn white and fall out. Then she'd be even uglier than me.

She huffed for a minute, then waved at me like she was saying good-bye. "It is hair. It will grow back." She turned to Titi Lola. "I have to talk to you. Alone."

Titi Lola pulled my smock off and kissed my forehead. "I think you a pretty girl." She dug into the pocket of her apron, pulled out a nickel, and motioned with her lips to the round gumball machine at the front of the salon. "Here. The green are my favorite. Sour apples."

Mamá took Titi Lola to the back, behind the curtain

where they kept the shampoos and pomades and chemical creams. They laughed, and I wondered if it was at me. The gumball machine choked on my nickel, and I had to give it a smack with my fist to get the ball out. I hit it twice more, even after I heard the gum roll down, just because. I got a blue. It filled up my mouth with sweetness and tinted my lips. I tried to sit with my back to the mirrors, but they boxed the room, and everywhere I turned, I caught sideways glimpses. I looked like a dirty American flag. My lips were blue, my ears and forehead prickled red, and my hair was white as the globe of a lightbulb. The women in the room gave me sympathetic smiles and tense grins, then looked away. I chewed hard on the gum and didn't smile back. I wanted to go home and hide from everyone.

When Mamá and Titi Lola came out, it was as if nothing had happened, as if they'd forgotten all about me.

"*Adios*, Lola. I will talk to you soon," Mamá said, and kissed her.

Titi Lola sighed and ran a hand over Mamá's arm. "Oh, Venusa." She turned to me, her eyes twinkling wet. "Verdita." She kissed my cheek. "You are such a lucky girl to have a new baby."

I wondered if Titi Lola was joking. I was certainly not lucky. I was probably the unluckiest girl on the whole island, on the whole earth!

On the drive home, Mamá didn't say one word. Instead she opened all the windows, turned on the radio, and hummed loud. The wind swirled through the jeep and tangled my hair into a crisscross of stiff gnarls even worse than the corkscrews. I tried to pull it back into a ponytail, but it was too short now and wouldn't stay put. So I sat with the coarse strands whipping in the breeze, leaving greasy lashes on my face. I would have liked it better if Mamá had yelled at me the whole ride home. Then I could be mad back, and I wouldn't think about my hair. But she didn't even care enough to do that.

Papi came up the grassy hill from the chicken coop when we got home. As soon as I stepped out of the car, he yelled, "Venusa! *Ay Dios! Madre Maria y los santos!*" He put his hands in the air and waved them around.

"Talk to your daughter. I had nothing to do with it," Mamá called back.

I was in for it good. But I was glad that Papi at least paid attention to me, unlike Mamá.

"Verdita! What is this? Why—how—your Titi Lola did this? Can you change it back?"

"I didn't know it would be so blond," I explained, and tucked my chin to my chest, hiding my face from him. I looked worse straight on.

"*Cristo!* Venusa, how could Lola do this to her? Did she go blind? Could she not see the mess she made? Why didn't you stop her?" Papi set his tools on the porch and put a hand on my shoulder. He was on my side.

"I wasn't there. Lola said that Verdita showed her a picture of what she wanted and said I knew. But no, I didn't."

Papi took his hand off my shoulder and grabbed my chin. His fingers smelled like chicken feed. The dirt made his grip like sandpaper.

"You lied, Verdita?" It was a question and a statement.

"Mamá never told me I couldn't," I tried. He didn't believe me. His eyebrows wrinkled.

"It's done now, Faro. No use punishing. Look at her! It's enough," Mamá said.

I was relieved not to be punished. I didn't want the belt.

"It's horrible," said Papi. Then I knew for sure that I was ugly, even to Papi, and the sting of the belt couldn't compare with that.

I tried to swallow the tears, to gulp them down into my belly. It didn't work. So I ran to my room and slammed the door. I grabbed my scissors, pulled the Simplicity picture from my pocket, and sliced the blond image into a pile of bits. That helped some, but my cheeks still burned; so I kicked off my shorts and underwear, sent them flying into the corners of my room. I laid the cold metal scissors against my warm private parts and snipped the thin, light hairs until every last one was gone. I didn't want to be anything like Mamá or Papi.

My blondness reflected in the mirror. I wished I'd never been born. I wished my soul had been put in another body, in the United States—not here on this island. Hot tears welled. I couldn't watch myself cry, my face all twisted and red beneath the white-blond haze, a ghoulish *vegigante*, a carnival queen. With all my might, I threw the scissors. The mirror shattered into a hundred little reflections—a hundred of me staring back at me. Hideous! Mamá and Papi burst into my room. They looked at the mirror, at the scissors on the floor, at me and my nakedness.

Mamá shoved Papi out of the room and covered me with her arms, even though I pushed her away, even though I told her I hated her.

*"Los pollitos dicen, pio, pio, pio . . ."* She sang the nursery rhyme she used to sing when I was a baby, the one that always made me feel like I was floating, safe in the magic of story-song. She held me there, singing, until my skin cooled—until the fire was smothered, and I could do no more than rest my head on her breast and sleep.

*Chapter Seven*

# An Explanation: Eve

F OR A FEW WEEKS I WORE A SCARF AROUND MY head to school, like Maria in *West Side Story*. Fredo called me a *bruja*, a witch, when I finally took it off. But I called him *cerdito*, to his face. That shut him up. Nobody else said anything. They were too busy talking about Rita Moreno, the first Puerto Rican to win an American Oscar. That news was even bigger than President Kennedy. I cut out magazine photographs of the whole cast and put them side by side in my journal.

By then, Mamá's baby bump showed through all her skirts. Every day, women from the *barrio* came with congratulatory bowls of *arroz con dulce* or *tembleque*. The sugar ants paraded from dish to dish. I didn't eat a bite. The women kiss-kissed my cheeks until I was covered with hot pink lipsticks and spit, and somebody always mentioned my hair. They sat around Mamá for hours, cooing over her belly like it had sprouted orchids. She loved it. I could tell. Sometimes women from church came with Señora Delgado. She was a *curandera*, a woman healer and a midwife, and gave Mamá gingerroot slivers to suck on, bags of powerful herbs to keep under her mattress, and an *azabache* bracelet to wear. Papi didn't like her. He said her medicine worked as good as spitting into the wind and calling it rain. I stayed away when the church group came to pray over the baby. I figured God already knew how I felt.

Papi shucked corn on the veranda. We had an early crop that year, and the spring rains kept the ears moist. We had to shuck them in a hurry or they'd spoil. I sat beside Papi on the bench, pulling brown, slimy leaves with raw fingers. From the rainwater, gnats made homes in the silky nests of the corn tips. They flew into my face when I ripped back the husks. I waved them away and flicked the rotten threads off my fingers. I wasn't very good at shucking, but it was better than being inside.

Señora Delgado led the group in prayer chants. Their sound echoed over the tiles in one long note. I wished we could play the radio to hush it. After finishing, they tottered down the road to the Florilla parish to pray some more and light candles before the Virgin Mary. Mamá tried to get me to come, but mass on Sundays was enough for me. She got no help from Papi. He went to church on *Nochebuena* and *Viernes Santo*, and for weddings, funerals, and baptisms when he was invited. Mamá went nearly every day. Twice when Señora Delgado came. As long as I didn't have to go, I was glad Mamá spent so much time in God's house and out of mine.

"Good corn." Papi held a cob to his nose and breathed in deep. "Sweet."

I put a cob to my nose and smelled the butter, like a promise. After all the green was peeled back, and the bugs and the dirt washed away, there was goodness.

I hadn't been alone with Papi since our trip to San Juan. It felt nice to be just us. "Papi, do you believe God hears us better in church or at home?" I asked.

He cleared his throat and scratched his nose with his thumb. "I think God hears us no matter where we are."

"That's why you don't go to church, like Mamá?"

"I don't need a priest to hear God. I hear him all the time when the wind blows through corn and sugarcane. You know that whistle?" Papi puckered his lips and blew a squeal. I knew it. He was good at whistling. Where Mamá was always reading and humming, Papi sucked his teeth and whistled.

"So, when you whistle while you read the newspaper, are you talking back to him?"

"Some days, Verdita. When your mamá is in a mood," Papi laughed. It made our bench jiggle. "We see God in different places, your mamá and I. Women need the church, you see." He tossed a cleaned ear into the pot of golden cobs.

"They do?" I wasn't a woman yet, but I would be some day, and it worried me that I'd have to spend my time sitting in the musty pews, my knees aching, my fingers cramped with holy beads.

"*Sí*, because of Eve," Papi said.

I didn't follow.

"Adam and Eve," Papi explained. "Everything in this world goes back to them, Verdita. When Eve bit the apple and handed it over to her husband, Adam, she created the first sin and she passed that guilt along to her daughter and her daughter's daughter, all the way down to Mamá. Women are always trying to purify themselves. That's why they go to church so much. While men, you see, we know that we were not the ones to pluck the apple from the tree." Papi pulled back the silk threads of his ear to find a brown hole. He broke off the wormy end and threw the rest into the pot, then continued, "And every woman's guilty apple is different."

I didn't have a guilty apple. I hadn't done anything wrong. If anyone should feel guilty, it was him and Mamá. There were lots of things they should feel guilty about, and I could list them easy. I sighed and kicked the basket with my toe. Obviously, Papi couldn't hear my spirit like he used to. Maybe he wasn't listening, maybe the new baby's spirit was talking to him now.

I slid my hand along my clean cob, healthy rows of yellow teeth. I wasn't going to spend my days in a moldy church, feeling guilty over things I didn't do. I didn't believe what Papi said about women, but I did believe what he said about hearing God. I heard God in the snap of peapods, smelled him in the banana leaves, saw him in the bright corn rows, and tasted him in every mouthful of bright white coconut. I didn't hear him in the church songs and sermons, and I had a feeling I never would.

*Chapter Eight*

# An Explanation: *Puta*

B y early June my hair had grown out some. Teline said I looked like an Oreo. I had to agree. Titi Lola bought the cookies at Walgreen's, and Teline ate a handful every afternoon; she carried them in a paper bag everywhere she went, and her teeth always looked like they had dirt stuck in the cracks. Oreos were from the States, more expensive than our island cookies. Papi didn't like the way they tasted. Too sweet. So I only got to eat them when I visited Teline and only when she had an extra.

That summer, when Omar came to visit, he brought his friend Blake with him. A few days before they arrived, Mamá bought a whole package of Oreos. She said she wanted to make Blake feel at home. But it wasn't his home, and I was annoyed at her for saying so. Before they arrived, I ate as many as I could and fed the rest to the goats.

When they finally came, Papi took one look at Omar and said he was becoming a man. He patted him on the back and smiled so wide I thought his eyes might disappear into his cheeks. He never smiled like that at me. He never noticed how I was growing. I looked Omar over. I didn't see a man. He was the same, but taller. So was I, though. He bragged about the dark hairs growing under his arm. Stuck his armpit in my face so I could see. Big deal. I didn't tell him that I had them too, between my legs. They grew back thick and dark after I cut them. I didn't show him mine, but I wanted to so he'd stop thinking he was so much more grown up. And he smelled funny. Deodorant, he said. Something called Right Guard. It was strong, like mouthwash; even after he left the room, I could still smell him.

The first night, after we pulled the boys' cots onto the porch and tented them in mosquito nets, we sat on the veranda eating fried chicken and *tostones*. With Blake there, we didn't fit at our table anymore. So we sat on the benches outside and held our plates in our laps, listening to Omar talk like he knew everything in the world. I wanted to remind him of what a coward he'd been the summer before, when we'd played Dare. I wanted to tell Blake how he'd whimpered in the dark outside the *jíbaros* bar. He might have forgotten that in the States, but I was here. I remembered everything.

"I want to be a baseball player," he announced, his mouth crunchy and slick. He wore a Yankees cap, and his eyes shone as black as beetles beneath.

"I'm going to practice all summer with Blake. We got all the stuff." He pulled a glove and some balls from his bag.

I didn't know much about baseball, but I knew you needed a bat, and I didn't see that in there. "Real baseball players have bats. You got one, or you plan to use a stick?"

Mamá frowned at me and Papi wrinkled his brow, but I didn't care. They could be mad, it didn't matter; they were having another baby anyhow.

"I got ten bats at home. They didn't fit in my suitcase." He eyed me from underneath his cap, then picked plantain from his teeth.

I missed Omar, but I couldn't tell him that. Not with Blake around. Not while he was acting all high and mighty. So, instead, I let how I felt about Mamá and Papi spill onto him. I didn't know how to feel about Blake yet. He was a guest, and I'd been raised not to be rude to guests. Family was one thing. They were part of you. You could hate your leg for cramping up or your eye for twitching. You could be mad all you wanted at your parts, but in the end, they were still there. You wouldn't be you if you cut them off. All the families in our *barrio* were related somehow, and the ones that weren't blood were at least Boricua. There weren't any strangers.

But Blake was a stranger to me, to my island, to everybody. I didn't want to like him. I tried to ignore him at first—speaking a mix of Spanish and English whenever he was nearby, so he wouldn't know what was going on. So he would know I knew more than he did. This was *my* home. He talked funny, too. Omar said he was from some‑ place called Amherst County in Virginia, and even though it was in the States, it was a lot like Puerto Rico. Blake grew up on a *finca* with chickens and goats and some of the same crops we had: corn and tobacco. He called his papi just plain "Pa" and it made me laugh every time he said it. His family had to sell their *finca* because they had bad crops, and his pa had to get work in the city driving a de‑ livery truck. That's how they ended up on Omar's street.

He was pale and blond and blue‑eyed and looked like the brother of the Simplicity girl I'd chopped up. The first day he was out in the sun, he burned blister‑red and Mamá broke every stem of the aloe vera plant to rub on his face and shoulders. He didn't cry, though, didn't make one sound when the bubbles oozed yellow and left pink holes in his skin. I'd never seen skin do that. Not Puerto Rican skin, at least. I wondered if it would grow back brown like mine, if he was shedding his old skin for island skin. When he first got burned, I was glad he was in pain, glad that my island sun had hurt him, but then he tanned over and his eyes shone brighter than before. He was changing, be‑ coming more Puerto Rican and less American. I wondered if that happened both ways.

But it wasn't just his outside that was different. When he first came, he was quiet and seemed afraid of every lit‑ tle lizard, every mound of ants, every rooster's crow. But after a few days he started talking more, laughing and yelling louder than the chickens. He caught lizards with his hands, dug up anthills with sticks, and told me stories, mostly about Amherst County—about the apple festival and the grocery stores with cold cow's milk in giant refrigerators. He'd never even tasted the powdered kind. When I showed him the can of Klim, he laughed and said, "That ain't milk! Whatever that is, it didn't come out of no cow, no goat either. Ain't you never seen a goat suckle its baby?" I had, but I never really thought about cow's milk until he told me.

"Zuck—zuck—zuck." He puckered his lips and sucked his cheeks. "It's like that." The wet redness of his tongue peeked out between his lips. An unexpected flutter caught beneath my ribs, and I went hot and cold. Sometimes, when I sat next to him, I felt funny like that—sweaty and frozen, like eating a *piragua*.

"Zuck—zuck—zuck." This time he crossed his eyes, and I laughed myself to tears.

Blake told me things I'd never known, and it wasn't like with Omar. He wasn't trying to be better than me. I could tell because I told him things too, and he listened. Like how to eat a passionfruit by cutting the top off and using a slice of sugarcane to spoon out the slippery seeds. Nothing tasted better in the world. Crunchy and smooth, sweet and sour. Blake and I ate almost the whole tree by ourselves. Omar didn't like them, which suited us just fine.

I liked being with Blake, just Blake. In my journal, I wrote down every story he told me so I could read it later and remember.


"You want to go swimming in the creek?" Omar asked one sticky afternoon.

Blake and I sat on the porch, licking passionfruit jelly off our fingers. Papi worked the farm, and Mamá lay inside, fat and lazy, watching the *telenovelas* with her feet up. That's all she did anymore.

"Yeah, let's go," I said.

Omar rolled his eyes. "I didn't ask you, skunk-girl." He turned to Blake.

There weren't any skunks in Puerto Rico, but Papi took me to see the movie *Bambi* at the *cine* hall a few years back. I knew what Flower looked like, and I tried to smooth back the black fuzzies at my temples, the blond ones in my ponytail. I didn't care if Omar called me a skunk, but when he said it in front of Blake, it stung.

"I don't know." Blake eyed me. "Why can't we all go swimming?"

Omar turned to me and narrowed his eyes under the lip of his cap. "I don't want to swim with Verdita. She'll make the water smell like *caca*. Skunk-girl."

"Shut up. I don't smell like *caca*. Butthead," I said. Blake had taught me English curse words, and I liked being able to use them with Omar—so he'd know I knew a thing or two.

"You do. All skunks stink! And you sure do look like a skunk to me." He laughed and gave Blake a punch to the arm.

"You stupid. *Idiota*," I said. He deserved both the English and the Spanish version.

Omar leaned forward like he was going to lay into me. I dug my heels into the ground, ready for it, but Blake interrupted, "My sister, Patsy—she bought a box of color from Safeway and dyed her hair exactly like Verdita's, only opposite—black at the end and blond at the top. I liked it. She's a beatnik. My ma and pa said she had to dye it back, so she left. That way she don't have to do what they say."

Omar pulled his cap over his eyes and picked the brown edges of a scab.

"You have a sister?" I asked. It was strange to think of him as a brother.

"She says she ain't never coming home 'cause she hates my pa," he went on. "He calls her a slut. I ain't seen her in three years." He stuck a piece of gutted passionfruit in his mouth and chewed.

Omar and I looked at him, but neither one of us said anything. The air moved through my nose, through the blades of grass across the yard, through the palm trees, through the whole island.

We had sluts in Puerto Rico, but I didn't know anybody that had one for a sister. Once in San Juan, a woman asked Papi for the time. She had rosy cheeks and red lips and her hair was curled in ringlets around her face. Mamá called her a *puta* and told her that she'd burn in hell. I thought she was the most beautiful woman I'd ever seen, an angel, and I nearly cried when I pictured her wings on fire.

I wanted someone to shut up the loud breeze. So I did. "Maybe Puerto Rico can make you forget, too."

Omar looked up, cocked his head to the side. Blake spat out the pinky rind.

"Huh? Don't be stupid, Verdita," said Omar.

"I'm not! If the States make you forget Puerto Rico, then maybe Puerto Rico can make you forget stuff in the States," I explained, but I could tell they didn't understand.

It made sense to me. Omar shook his head and rolled his eyes. Blake smiled.

"Come on. I'm hot," said Omar. He hopped off the porch and started across the lawn. Blake and I followed.

"I think you're right, Verdita," Blake said when Omar was far enough ahead and couldn't hear.

I nodded. I knew I was. He put his hand on my shoulder and squeezed it hard. It hurt a little, but I liked the way his sticky fingers pressed into my skin. Cold chills spilled down my back. I wished he would do it again, but he didn't. We walked barefoot through the tangled grass, the sun making his skin buttery, and I wished the yard would go on forever. I wished we could stay there, in between places—between the leaving and the coming.

We marched into the brush behind the chicken coop and lay belly-down in the shallow creek, our stomachs suctioned into the gooey mud, the waters running over our backs, the conversation roving like the current.

Blake couldn't stop talking about the day before, when Mamá took the boys with her to buy boxes of *con-flei* and cans of powdered milk at the *tienda*. It was Blake's first time in the main plaza of Florilla.

"It was crazy," he said. "A man walked right down the street with a sword!"

"A machete," Omar corrected. He yanked a fern blade from the bank, placed it between his thumbs, and blew fart sounds.

"Papi has a machete," I said, and dug a hole in the mud with my finger. The dirt puffed into a cloud and swirled off on the current.

"Everybody at home has a gun, and everybody here has a machete," Omar said. He flipped over and leaned against the creek bank. The water filled his shorts like a giant blue jellyfish. He lifted his arm and craned his neck around. "Hey, I got a couple more." He ran his fingers beneath his armpit. "See?" He pulled it close to Blake.

"Cool, man." Blake laughed. His voice rippled my skin.

Omar leaned his pit toward me, holding his arm over his head like a gorilla.

"Get that out of my face." I smacked him away. "*Ay Dios*. You think you're so grown up. Everybody's got hairs on their body." I flipped over and propped up on my elbows. The water cleaned the mud off my front, tickling my stomach and thighs. "I got them too. So what?" I scissor-kicked the water; it made little *pu-plunk* sounds, but no splash.

"You don't have hairs. I've seen under your arms." Omar crossed his arms over his bare chest, like he knew so much. "Besides, girls don't get hairs. Only men."

"My sister Patsy had hair on her arms and legs. She shaved it off with Pa's razor every morning," said Blake. He sat up in the creek, his waist and legs swallowed by the water, his chest slick and sand-colored.

"See! That's how much you know." I stuck out my tongue at Omar.

"Liar. Show us, then," Omar said. He lay back in the creek and let the water lift his body to the surface, weightless.

"I'm not a liar," I said, but Omar couldn't hear. His ears were underwater. I grabbed his leg and pushed it so his face dipped beneath the surface. He bobbed back up, surprised and angry.

"What are you doing? You could have drowned me!"

"I'm not a liar," I repeated.

I knew I shouldn't, but I stood, unlooped my arms, and in one quick motion rolled my bathing suit off. It slid down my thighs and over my knees into the water. I stood naked before them, my legs apart, my hands on my hips. "See." I eyed my private parts. The wet kinks seemed darker in the outdoor light, and even I was a bit surprised. My body was entirely different now that someone else saw it. There were the two guava berries I'd felt in Titi Lola's salon, swollen and brown-nippled, my navel and the patch of coarse curls. The rest of my body seemed to disappear.

My eyes met Blake's.

"Verdita!" Omar yelled. "Cover yourself!"

He reached his hand across Blake's face. Blake turned away. And then I felt what Papi spoke of. The guilty apple. I felt Eve's sin. But I didn't want to be like Mamá and all the other women in history, so I fought against it.

"I don't have to do what you say," I told Omar. My hands and legs ached to cover up, to shield myself, to run into the brush and hide, but I wouldn't. Not yet. Not until I decided and not because Omar told me to.

"Slut! That's what they do—take off their clothes." Omar splashed his way out of the creek and up the bank. "Come on, Blake!"

Blake followed behind, his eyes downcast. He wouldn't look at me.

I didn't know that about sluts. And I wondered if Mamá was a slut, bare-chested on the couch with Papi. My arms shook as I pulled my bathing suit up. I still felt naked even after I was dressed. A hot sob caught in my throat. I thought I might throw up.

They'd gone toward the house. I panicked, climbed up the bank, and ran after them. If Omar told Mamá and Papi! I ran as fast as I could, the branches scratching my skin, my toes squishing in jungle mud and moss, until I reached the grass of our yard. There I stopped. Mamá would be yelling already if Omar had told. The only sound was a chicken squawking. I wondered how long we'd been gone. Were the *telenovelas* still on, or was Mamá making dinner? The chicken shrieks grew louder than usual. I circled the coop and, coming around the side, found Mamá with a black hen on her lap, her fingers around its neck.

"*Pollo*, stop fighting me," she said. The chicken pecked and scratched, squawked and flapped, but Mamá held it firm. She gave a hard twist, and its wings slowed like an angel landing. "There," Mamá sighed, and jiggled the neck to make sure it was broken. She looked at me. "*Arroz con pollo*. This chicken's all grown. Ready for my pot." She stood and wiped her forehead. Her eyes narrowed on me.

My knees shook. I wrapped my arms around my body. I knew she could see right through the material, right through to my nakedness and shame. There was no place to hide.

"Verdita?" Mamá held the limp chicken on her hip; its wings flapped in slow motion.

The hen's eyes were wide and unblinking, like the roosters in Papi's study. Mamá came closer with it. I backed away. The black wings moved up and down, up and down. The red comb flopped to the side. The dark eyes watched me. They knew what I'd done.

"What's wrong?" Mamá set the dying chicken on the ground and took my hands in hers. They were soft, like I remembered.

"Mamá…" I let her hold me. I held her too, pulling her close and burying my face in her neck, hidden in the familiar smell and darkness. For that moment, nothing else mattered.

She rubbed my back. "Tell me," she said. And I wanted to. If this was Eve's sin, then Mamá would understand.

"I—I was naked and they saw me," I whispered. The shame sliced my throat and I pushed my face harder against her skin.

Mamá stopped rubbing and went stiff, then lifted my face to hers. Her eyes were flat, like stale cups of coffee. "Go dry yourself and dress. I'll come soon." She let go of me before I was ready and turned back to the hen in the grass thumping in a circle, dying with every moment.

INSIDE, I DRIED myself, braided my hair, dressed, and waited. The house was silent. Empty. I hated being that alone. And I began to wish that I hadn't told Mamá what I'd done. Omar and Blake hadn't told her. She would never have known. I sucked on the wet curlicue at the bottom of my braid.

The door hinges squeaked when she entered. The secret way she slipped into my room made my hands shake. I balled them up and dug my fingernails into my palms. She took a seat beside me on the bed.

"We were swimming," I began, but then stopped. I didn't want Eve's guilt, even if I had it.

"Verdita," Mamá said. She unballed my fist and stroked it like she was saying good-bye. My fingertips went numb.

"What I am about to tell you is very important." Mamá sighed. "You can't let boys touch you, or see you uncovered. Being with a boy like that is a sin. Have you heard the word *puta*?" She whispered it even though I'd heard it before. That's what she'd called the red-lipped angel in San Juan, what Omar called me in the creek.

I nodded.

"Do you know what a *puta* is?"

A slut. A prostitute. Women who wore bright makeup and curled their hair and took off their clothes. "*Sí,* Mamá," I said.

"They are sinful. They let men see them uncovered. If you let boys do that to you, people will think you are one of them. And, even worse, you could get pregnant. You will be a *señorita* soon, once the monthly bleeding starts."

Bleeding? I tried to take in a breath, but my lungs cramped. Mamá stroked my fingers.

"There was a woman many years ago, before I was a *señorita*. All the men liked her because she was the most beautiful *señorita* in the *barrio*. She was engaged to a handsome, wealthy man and everyone admired the couple. But then, on her wedding night, the truth was revealed. The white sheets were not stained. Do you know what that means?"

I didn't.

"When you get married, your wedding sheets will be stained with a little blood from your private parts. It proves to your husband that you are pure. That no other man has seen you under your clothes."

I remembered Blake's wide eyes at the creek.

"There was no stain. The woman was not pure. Her husband was furious, and that very night he took her back to her father's house. He did not want her. When her father discovered that she was not a virgin, he threw her out too."

I felt sick to my stomach. I didn't want Papi to throw me out.

"She was a *puta* in the slums of San Juan. She was pregnant seven times, each with a different man, until she died of sickness. It was terrible." Mamá crossed herself. I did too.

"I tell you this so that you do not make these mistakes—so you don't end up like your cousin Delia with a bastard child inside of you and the man responsible run off." She patted my hand and shook her head.

My chest tightened. Delia was pregnant? I thought about her and Carlos, pictured Carlos's hands around her waist, his face black against her neck. I wondered if Teline had told.

"Whatever you were doing at the creek," Mamá continued, "you must never do again. I won't tell your papi if you promise."

I didn't want to be a *puta*. I didn't want to bleed and die. "I promise," I said.

If Delia was a *puta*, then what about Mamá? Since

pregnancy was the punishment, she must have been a *puta* with Papi! Was it the same in the States? Did Blake's sister let men see her without clothes on? Had she ever been pregnant? I wrapped my arms around my stomach. Blake saw me, and I liked it. But I didn't want to get fat and lazy and pregnant like Mamá.

"Good." Mamá stood. "So tomorrow we go to church. You must repent, Verdita. I don't want sinfulness in my house. "

I knew there was a price to pay. And I wished even more that I hadn't confessed to Mamá. Now she had something to use against me.

"But can't I repent here?" I asked.

Mamá shot me a look. *"Ay, Dios mio."* She crossed herself. "You think God is that easy to please?"

I didn't think it was easy to please God, but I didn't think it was hard, either. And besides all that, I didn't want to be like Delia and Mamá, spending good summer days in a cold church. I wasn't yet a *señorita*.

"It's not fair," I whined.

Mamá shook her head. "Fair? Was Christ on the cross fair? Was—" She stopped and winced, then rubbed her belly. She took a few deep breaths, and when she spoke again, her voice was pinched and slow. "You *will* confess to Padre Ramos."

Mamá was swollen and lazy and full of rules even she didn't follow. Her soft paunch had grown round and hard, like she'd swallowed a whole pumpkin. It reminded me of

the story Papi told about how Puerto Rico became an island.

Back before Mamá and Papi were born, before my
*abuelos*, before their *abuelos*, Puerto Rico was a mountain
in the middle of a giant, grassy plain. That was a fact. The
original Taino people loved their mountain home, but
needed shade and trees for shelter, so they planted a handful of magic seeds and a thick forest grew. A vine with a
beautiful golden flower sprang out of the ground and
turned into a pumpkin. Two Taino men found it and began
to argue over who could take it home. In their struggle,
the pumpkin fell, rolled down the mountain and split
open on a rock. Water poured out and covered the valley,
forever making Puerto Rico an island, alone in the middle
of the sea.

I wondered what life would be like if Puerto Rico was
still a mountain. Then I could climb down and walk to the
States, leave this place. The ocean wouldn't stand in between.

Fine. I'd go to church. But I'd tell Padre Ramos a thing
or two about Mamá, and the sin growing inside her. I
hated that bump, that swollen pumpkin. I wished I could
throw it down the mountain, let it split open, let the waters run back to the sea.

## Chapter Nine

# Repentance

THE NEXT MORNING, MAMÁ WOKE ME EARLY. "Put on the dress I made with the *maga* buds. We're leaving in five minutes," she said.

I was willing to go to Padre Ramos and confess for acting like a *puta*, but I was too close to being a *señorita* for Mamá to tell me what clothes to wear. So I pulled out a purple dress with a scalloped neckline and moved the *maga* dress to the back behind all the others.

Mamá came back and saw my outfit. "This is not a party," she snapped, and riffled through my closet until she found it. "Here. And *no* crinoline."

Without the crinoline, the bell skirt hung limp, like a deflated balloon. I swore I'd never wear that pink print. It reminded me of everything I wasn't. But I was already in enough trouble, and I didn't want my repentance to last more than a day. So I stuck my arms through the holes and yanked it over my head. It still smelled of starch and chalk and the rice-paper pattern. I clipped back the hair around my face and didn't bother to look in the mirror. I knew what I'd see: ugliness, through and through, and that was fine. Even though I didn't like going to church, it was the one place where being pretty was shameful, so I fit in just right. Being ugly was a virtue. The nuns were proof of that.

At the kitchen table, the boys looked up from their bowls of *con-flei* and then continued to slurp from their spoons. It was the first time I'd seen them since the creek. I avoided their eyes. Papi read the newspaper.

"Good morning, Verdita," he said without putting down *La Primera Hora*.

"Morning," I whispered.

Mamá had promised not to tell him, but she'd proven herself a liar in the past. Papi read his paper and drank his *café con leche*, slow and even, like every morning. He didn't know. If he did, he'd have already thrown me out of the house. I wondered what lie Mamá made up to explain my trip to confession. I balled up my fists just thinking about it. I wished I could go back to the day before and shove a handful of creek mud in my mouth.

Nobody spoke. The boys slurped; the newspaper crunched and Mamá sat on the kitchen stool, loudly beating a broom against the floor. When she saw me, she flipped it over, cinched the handle between her thighs, and wrapped an old rag around the head.

"Why is Mamá beating the broom?" I asked Papi. Mamá heard.

"Sin comes with an evil spirit. I want it out of my house," she replied. And even though she spoke to me, she faced Omar and Blake. Their eyes were fixed on their spoons.

Mamá set the broom on its handle behind the open front door, pinched salt from the salt box, and tossed it over the broom head, then pinched more and tossed it toward the boys, then again at me. I flinched.

This was an old Puerto Rican tradition. A wrapped broom behind the door made unwanted visitors leave; it always worked. I'd seen Mamá do it when nosy neighbors came to visit, but she'd never done it to family. Never to blood relatives. The broom stood tall, propped up against the doorknob like a thin ghost. I prayed this one time it wouldn't work. I didn't want it to sweep me out, Blake and Omar either. While Mamá got her purse, I pinched a little salt and prayed that instead of us, the broom would sweep out the baby. I spit on the grains to make them stick to the broom head, to make it more powerful than Mamá's magic, and threw them on.

"Let's go." Mamá pulled her purse over her shoulder.

I walked quickly past the broom without looking at it, and made sure that mine was the last pinch to be thrown before we left.

THE CHURCH WAS silent, suffocating. When we entered, Mamá dipped her fingers in the bowl of holy water and crossed herself. I did the same, though the water always made my fingers smell like *escabeche*, pickled fish. There was only one Catholic church in Florilla, the Parish of the Saints. It had a gold, green, and red altar that stood as tall as the church steeple, with a statue of Christ staring blankly out over the pews. I didn't mind the Christ statue as much as the Virgin Mary one. She made my scalp prickle. Her skin was pale and her robes hung over her head in white sheets, like giant gloved hands in prayer. The sun-crown behind her head fanned out in spikes of gold, bronzed knives splintering out. Everyone said she was beautiful, like a doll, but she scared me most of all: eyes forever down-cast, silent lips glued together.

Mamá pushed me along to the confessional booths. Black whispering boxes. Usually I made up stuff when I went in, not wanting to bore Padre Ramos on the other side of the lacy window. None of my sins were too bad, though, just sinful enough to be interesting: disobeying Mamá, not saying prayers, pulling the tails off lizards, eating too much candy, not making my bed. A couple of rosaries and I was forgiven. But this was different. I wondered what it would take for God and the Virgin Mary, and Papi and Mamá, to love me again.

"You tell him everything." Mamá opened the flap and pushed me inside the blackness.

The box smelled like the gray smoke they puffed over

us during mass. It made my nose run. I took a seat on the wooden slat. The latch creaked and slid open to show the pores in the lace.

"My child," said Padre Ramos, "what have you to confess?" I liked Padre Ramos's voice. It sounded like the ocean. Sometimes during mass, I closed my eyes and it nearly put me to sleep.

"In the name of the Father and of the Son and of the Holy Spirit," I began. "My last confession was two weeks ago because my cousin Omar and his friend Blake—he's from the United States—have been visiting and I haven't had time. But Mamá has been coming for our family. She comes almost every day, but it's hard because she's pregnant and her feet are fat and hurt and—" I was rambling. I didn't want to tell him yet. I had to work up to it.

"Padre," I whispered. Mamá shuffled outside the box. "I ..." I didn't know how to start it off. It was my first truly big sin to confess.

Padre Ramos leaned in and pressed the side of his head against the window. Little black hairs stuck through the lace. "Take your time, child. It'll be all right. *Papá Dios* already knows your heart. Just tell me what happened."

I scooted up to the window and cupped my hand around my mouth. "I took off my bathing suit in the creek." There. It was out. I went on, "I only did it because Omar was bragging about his stupid armpit hairs. I wanted to show him that everybody has hair."

"So you uncovered your body before your cousin and his friend?" He said it as a statement, not a question.

The Simplicity dress suddenly felt too small, and I tugged at the neck to get air. I hadn't told Padre about Blake. I eyed the curtain flap, wanting to kick it and send Mamá flying back into the pew like a ball. She must have told him—called him or sent him a secret message.

Or maybe God had told him. I scooted back from the window.

"*Sí*. But I had to." I picked at my dress seams, pulling the stitches of the blooms apart. "He called me a liar. I had to prove I wasn't."

"Did they ask you to unclothe yourself?" Padre asked.

"No. I did it 'cause I wanted to," I said firmly.

He cleared his throat. "Verdita, just because you want something doesn't make it right. That's why God gave us the Ten Commandments and the Bible. To help us know what we can and cannot do. Lust is one of the seven deadly sins."

But I hadn't lusted.

"No, Padre—" I began.

"It is a desire of the body, Verdita." He cut me off. "And the Lord tells us to treat our bodies as temples. We must not abuse what He has given us. And God sees every, thing."

A deadly sin. Desire of the body. He spoke in riddles! Besides, if God was all-knowing, then he knew I didn't lust. I did it to show Omar. I did it because I was right, and I didn't have to explain that to Padre Ramos, Mamá, or anybody. God knew. I yanked hard on a thread hanging from the hem and it split the seam open.

Padre Ramos went on, but I stopped listening. Mamá had told me that sometimes men talked to hear themselves, like when Papi lectured us on politics or the correct way to get eggs from under the chicken. I figured it worked the same for priests.

I remembered the Elvis Presley song. I could almost hear Señora Alonzo's mandolin playing outside the confessional, and I tapped my feet to the rhythm.

"You are a good girl, Verdita. You don't want to be stained with sin."

He sighed deep, and I didn't know if I was supposed to say something. His breath was heavy and whistled through his nose. I sniffed up the drips running out of mine and wished he'd blow his. He continued, "You must repent of this sin. You must promise never to do it again. You want to be clean and pure, *sí*?"

Again, his nose whistled.

"Verdita?" He leaned into the lace.

"*Sí*, Padre," I replied. It was easier not to argue. I couldn't make him understand the truth.

"*Bueno*. Do six Hail Marys and six Our Fathers for penance. Anything else to confess?"

Now it was my turn to point the finger.

"*Ay* Padre," I sighed and propped my elbows on the ledge of the window. "It's about my mamá and papi."

I wouldn't tell him how I wanted to kick Mamá in the stomach and roll her down the mountain, or that I'd written that I hated her in my journal. Hating people was a huge sin, and I already had enough Hail Marys. This was my chance to set the holy record right.

"You must obey and respect your parents. That's in the Bible," Padre said.

He took their side before I'd even explained.

"I try, but, Padre, they are liars. *They* are the sinful and wicked ones. Why doesn't God punish them?" The words came out steamy and filled up the box.

"Why do you say your parents are liars? I know your mamá and papi well." He didn't know how they really were, not like I did. He didn't live with us.

"Padre, they do bad things together," I whispered.

"What things?" Padre whispered back.

Here it was—the undeniable proof. "I saw them one night on the couch. Without their clothes on—naked!" I widened my eyes so he could see I was telling the truth.

"Oh," he said, and shifted away from the window.

That's all? Maybe he misheard. I went on, "Lust." I used his word.

"Verdita, what you saw your mamá and papi doing was natural. Ask your mamá to explain it and you'll see. It isn't sinful. It's a part of God's plan, and now your mamá is going to have a baby. Be happy! You have a little brother or sister coming."

I shook my head. How could it be sinful for me and

natural for them? The tips of my ears burned, and I had to bite my tongue to keep from crying out just how unfair Padre's rules were—how unfair God's rules were!

"I pray that the Virgin will protect you and guide your mind and actions," he said.

The Virgin Mary couldn't help me. I wasn't anything like her, and I never would be. I rubbed the sweat off my nose with my fallen hemline and kicked the confessional wall. Fine, I just wanted out of there.

I let the words I'd been taught run off my tongue. "I am sorry for these and all the sins of my past life." And I was sorry. Sorry to be stuck in that black cage. Sorry to smell like sour fish. Sorry to be a girl in Puerto Rico. I was sorry for a lot of things. God understood that, even if nobody else did.

Padre Ramos said some words of forgiveness, and I crossed myself when I thought I should. It was almost over.

"Give thanks to the Lord, for he is good," he said.

"For his mercy endures forever." I reached for the curtain flap. "Amen." I flung it shut behind me.

Mamá knelt just outside on a pew, pretending to be caught up in her own prayers.

"Mamá," I said.

"Ay! Verdita!" She acted startled. I rolled my eyes. She didn't need to pretend to me. She'd been standing next to the curtain flap the entire time. I had smelled her rose perfume. It stood out from the gray smoke and the *escabeche* stink of my fingers.

"So? Are you right with *Papá Dios?*" she asked.

"I have penance."

"Sit down and start. And when you are done, you will pray until I say it is time to leave." She pulled me down beside her and handed over her rosary beads. They were hot from her hands, each bead worn past the dark shine of the wood varnish to the lightness beneath. I guessed if you prayed hard enough and long enough, you could even change the color of wood.

I knelt before the Christ altar and said my Hail Marys and Our Fathers as fast as I could, the lines rolling into one another until I couldn't hear the individual words anymore. They changed into something else, vibrations over my tongue, magic that made my mouth tingly and my head light. Beside me, Mamá's swollen body swayed to the rhythm of her prayers, her mouth moved but no words came out; her eyes were closed like the Virgin Mary's. Mamá was like her. I could see that.

I squeezed my eyes tight until shapes formed and moved under my lids, and I wondered if those were the saints that we couldn't see with open eyes. Pray. I was supposed to pray, but I heard Elvis in my head. I tried to hush his voice by concentrating on the hard beads in my fist, and the magic worked because the singing quieted, and I was left alone with my voice.

I prayed that God would punish Omar—make his hair or teeth fall out, turn his toes green, or give him *solitaria* crawling inside his belly. He deserved to be punished, too, for calling me a liar and a slut. But instead, he sat at home eating *con-flei*. He could say whatever he wanted and nobody cared, because he was a boy. They all liked boys better, even God. The Virgin Mary had Jesus, not Jesusa.

If Mamá's baby was a boy, I'd be blamed for everything bad in our house, just like Teline. So I prayed that God would make the baby a girl. Lastly, I prayed that Blake would be my best friend instead of Omar's, and if Mamá and Papi stopped loving me, I could go to the States and live with him.

I was out of things to talk to God about, so I peeked through the fuzziness of my lashes, and watched the candle flames flicker beneath the Virgin statue. I didn't expect much from my prayers. They were as good as wishing into seashells.

When I was little, at the beach in Aguadilla, I found a shimmery pink shell that curled around itself like the inside of a gardenia. It was the most beautiful thing I had ever seen. Papi said shells that perfect belonged to the Ocean King, and if I made a wish into it and threw it back to the water, it would make its way to the sea castle. If the wish was worthy, if the Ocean King felt that it came from a pure heart, then he'd grant it. I spent months collecting shells, making wishes and throwing them off the shores of Puerto Rico. None of them ever came true. I stopped believing in seashell wishes when I saw a crab crawl out of one, and Señora Alonzo explained where they came from in science class. Papi lied. Just like he lied about other things.

I squeezed my hands together, the prayer beads digging into my palms. I wanted to leave. My knees ached. But Mamá still knelt, swayed, and mouthed words next to me. Being in church was worse than Papi's belt or lectures.

By the time we left, my stomach growled and gurgled, and I felt weak. I hadn't eaten breakfast. Mamá said we were fasting until I repented. Now that I had, I craved the *chicharrones* I smelled on the breeze. An old woman on the corner was frying pork skin and selling bags of it for a dollar.

"I'm hungry," I said. "Can I get some *chicharrones* for the ride home?"

Mamá eyed the woman and licked her lips. She wanted some too, I could tell. Since the baby started to grow inside her, she was always eating. Today she'd gone hours with just wooden beads to suck on.

"Now that you've repented." She rubbed her belly, then fished a dollar from her purse.

I paid the old woman at the corner, and she gave me a paper bag pocked in grease.

"*Chicharrones* for the pretty girl," the old woman said.

Me—with my floppy dress and dyed hair? I looked around. I was alone.

"Your mamá is lucky to have such a beautiful daughter." She smiled. She had missing teeth and a wrinkled face, but her eyes were sky blue and almond-shaped. I thought she must have been beautiful a long time ago.

The fryer crackled, and she went back to fishing skins

out of the hot oil. I stood for a moment, not wanting to leave, and wishing she'd spoken in front of Mamá—to remind her that I was good and some people could see it.

We ate the bag on the drive home, both of us licking our fingers clean of the oil and salt.

At the bottom of our driveway, Mamá put the jeep in park. "Promise me you won't do that again," she said. Crumbs sprinkled her belly like she'd been blessed with holy *chicharrones*. "You will be a *señorita* soon. You must be careful, Verdita."

I was too tired to argue and too full to talk any more about sin and God, lust and repentance. So I nodded.

Mamá pulled my head to her chest. "You're a good girl," she said. I didn't push away. Even though I thought I ought to. I missed the way it felt to be close to her. And this time neither one of us let go for a long while. I wondered if she'd heard the old woman, or if the prayer beads actually worked better than seashells.


After we got home, I sat alone behind the house with a basket of corn ears between my knees. Papi had harvested five more baskets and left them on the veranda. There was a cockfight at the *jíbaros* bar, and he'd gone with Tío Benny. I tried not to think about it. It had already been a long day of thinking. So I shucked. I'd gotten good at it. I liked the way the threads slipped between my fingers like my hair underwater, the way the yellow kernels lined up neat and even and smelled green and clean. Mamá was going to make *sorullo de maíz* that night. It was one of my favorites.

From down the side of the hill, Omar and Blake came carrying their baseball and gloves and shouting over who threw the farthest. They stopped talking when they saw me.

"Hey." Omar nodded and took off his Yankees cap. I hadn't seen him capless since the summer before. His hair was long and shaggy; dark curls stuck, wet with sweat, to his forehead. He took a seat next to me on the bench. I could smell his Right Guard and something sour, like he'd bathed in holy water.

"We were talking today and..." He hung his cap on his knee and ran his hand through his hair. It stuck up and stayed that way. "You shouldn't have done what you did." He tapped my basket with his glove. "But I'm sorry I called you a slut. So that's all." He eyed Blake and stood. "I got first bath." The back door banged shut behind him.

I picked up an ear and ripped the husk from the cob.

Blake sat down beside me and reached into my basket. "I used to do this with Ma all the time. Patsy never liked the farm. She'd give me money to do her chores. Back before," he said. He skillfully pulled the leaves. He was good at it and started on another ear before I was done with mine.

"You miss your sister?" I asked.

He shrugged. "Sometimes I can barely remember the jokes she told. I write them down so I don't forget."

He pulled hard on the silk, then stopped and turned to me. "You aren't a slut. Omar was wrong to say it." Corn threads webbed his fingers, and he gently picked at them until they caught on the breeze and flew away. "I'll help you shuck. I don't mind."

"Thanks," I said. I wanted my last prayer to come true— for Blake to be my best friend. I wanted God to give me a sign that he'd heard me, that I was worthy of my wishes.

Blake reached into the basket to take another, and when he did, his hand brushed across the inside of my thigh, rough knuckles against my soft skin. My legs went stiff and shaky. My knees buckled in tight against the basket weave, and it was a good thing I was already sitting down because I would have fallen right over. Down low and deep, a burning tickle spread outward until my whole body was a fever. I tried to keep my hands moving, to hide from Blake what I knew for sure he could see, a glaze of goosebumps and sweat. It was like the feeling I had when Teline kissed my neck, only bigger. I wished I could feel it again until my whole body caught fire or froze, whichever.

It didn't seem as scary now—what Delia and Carlos did under the mango tree, what Mamá and Papi did on the couch. Maybe Padre Ramos was right about it being natural. I reimagined Blake's touch over and over while we shucked, the earthy corn smell around us, the light changing to dark.

## Chapter Ten

# The Chupacabra

THE DAY BEFORE OMAR AND BLAKE FLEW BACK to the States, Tío Benny and Titi Ana came for a good-bye dinner. Titi Lola couldn't come. She had a late-night perm on Doña Guerrero, who'd just moved to our *barrio*. A Cuban family. They were the first Cubans in our mountain town, and it bothered me that I didn't know everybody anymore. The town was changing. Strangers were coming and going.

Tío Benny played a lonesome melody on his guitar while we sat with empty plates and stripped cobs at our sides.

"Who wants to hear a story?" Tío Benny stopped his strumming. "How about a scary one?" He handed his guitar to Titi Ana. The adults pulled their chairs close while we scooted to his feet and sat pretzel-legged. Two things Tío Benny did better than anybody else: sing and tell stories.

"What should I tell?" he asked.

"A good pirate story," Mamá replied.

"No, tell them about the Chupacabra," Papi laughed.

"What's the Chupacabra?" asked Blake.

"*Ay, sí,* the Chupacabra," Tío Benny scratched his head. "Do you think it is wise—on such a dark night? I hear that even mentioning it on nights like these ... you know, the jungle hears everything."

I scooted close to Blake. My knee grazed his. The Chupacabra was a monster that lived deep in the rain forests of the island. Everybody in Puerto Rico knew that.

"Some say it is nothing but a child's tale—but I tell you, I've seen the work of the beast, and once you've seen it, you believe. Right, Faro?"

"*Sí,* Benny," said Papi.

Titi Ana snickered beside Mamá. Papi lit the mosquito torches around the porch, then poured another short glass of gin and took a seat. The firelight cast an orange glow over Tío Benny's face; his eyes were black as papaya seeds.

"One day when I was twelve years old and Faro was fifteen, we were walking through the jungle, bringing sacks of coffee beans back to the farm. Our mule, Zapato, moved slow. He was an old, stubborn donkey. Faro pulled him along by the bit and I walked behind, thwacking his hind end with the flat side of the machete, but still he moved like a water slug. The trip took nearly twice as long as usual, and before we knew it, night had come, and we were pushing our way through darkness, chopping vines with our machetes, and praying we were headed in the right direction.

"Suddenly, Zapato, who had never broken his pace, reared like the devil was in him and took off through the jungle. He left so quickly that we couldn't see which direction to follow. Then—I'll never forget it as long as I live—the coquís went silent, and in the distance we heard a terrible howling, like a pig being slaughtered."

"Oh, Benny!" Mamá shook her head. "They are children," she reminded him.

I gripped my ankles. Next to me, Blake's arms flexed; his breath came shallow and quick.

Tío Benny went on, "Faro and I began to run away as fast as we could, thrashing the darkness with our machetes." He sliced his arm through the air. "The jungle tearing at our clothes." He pulled at his shirt. "The howling growing louder and louder. Nearer and nearer."

I put my hands over my ears.

"Then. I fell."

We gasped.

"The howling was right on top of me, and I knew I could not escape. I thought those were my last moments on earth. I turned to see the monster's face—" Tío Benny stopped and crossed himself. *"Ay Dios mío!"*

*"Ay Dios mío,"* I whispered, not knowing what it was he saw, but imagining a great many horrors.

"There, hovering above me, were two glowing red eyes. The Chupacabra! Come to suck my blood and leave me white as a ghost!"

We all gasped again.

"You'll give them nightmares," Mamá said. "Faro, please."

"Benny is the one telling the story, Venusa. I have nothing to do with it." He took another sip of his gin.

The mountain jungle around our house seemed darker than before. I scooted closer to Blake. My skin felt like it was covered with a million mosquitoes, and I scratched at my arms and legs until they were red with nail tracks.

Tío Benny winked at Titi Ana, then continued. "And just as I knew it would lay its teeth into me, just as the hot breath of death warmed my face, there was a light. The brightest light I've ever seen." He paused. "And the red eyes vanished back into the jungle."

"What was it?" I asked.

"It was your papi. He'd found his way out and come back with a lantern and Abuelo. He saved me."

Papi raised his gin to Tío Benny and laughed. "I would not let the devil feast on you, Benny."

"I am grateful!" said Tío Benny. Then he reached out his arm to the black night and shook his head. "Never doubt the legends of the jungle, children."

I bit my lower lip.

"Enough, Benny," Titi Ana said. "They won't sleep a wink."

"Is it true?" asked Omar.

"*Sí.* It's true," said Tío.

"Who wants some more *arroz con dulce?*" Mamá pulled herself up, belly first, from the chair.

"No more Chupacabra talk. Play something happy, Benny. It's the boys' last night," said Titi Ana, and she followed Mamá into the kitchen.

"I tell you no lies," he said. "I'll never forget that night." I knew I wouldn't either. He picked up his guitar. "Let's get you boys ready for America! How about 'La Bamba'? Richie Valens, man." The fast strum broke the silence.

He did his best rocker impression, and we clapped and laughed and, for a while, forgot about the red eyes of the Chupacabra. But later that night, while Mamá and Papi snored next to each other and Omar and Blake slept side by side on their netted cots, I lay alone with the sheets pulled up to my neck, the shadows dancing around the door and over the bumpy mounds on my bed. The howling sound Tío Benny spoke of wailed in the wind, the shimmer of his black eyes winked at me through the slats of my window. I tried to be brave, tried to ignore the sounds and sleep; but then there was a creak or a swish, and I'd sit up in bed, gripping my sheets.

We'd said "Chupacabra" out loud. It had to have heard us. And now it was coming to drink my blood and make me white! I thought of Dick and Jane, and Blake when he'd first arrived, of Mamá's neck and the bloodless victims of the devil's feast. I wanted my skin to turn white like the men and women in the States, but not pale as death. I pulled the sheets over my head and prayed that the monster would eat all the chickens in the coop and be full before it reached our house. The window sill creaked. I opened my eyes beneath the covers. My hot breath filled up the space and choked me. I had to come out; I had to get air. But the Chupacabra—it could be right there, on the other side, waiting to bite. I imagined blood seeping out of my private parts like Mamá said, and the monster drinking the stream until I was empty. I cupped my hand between my legs and willed the blood to stay inside. Something billowed the sheets. The Chupacabra? Or even worse, maybe Teline tattled and Carlos had come in darkness to snatch me from my bed and make me a San Juan *puta*!

I kicked at the covers as hard as I could and ran to Mamá and Papi's room. At the door, I stopped, afraid of turning the doorknob. But Padre Ramos said it was all natural. I thought of Teline kissing my neck, of Blake's hand over my thigh and the way my body looked, wet and warm in the creek. I looked back to my room, more afraid of what I imagined than what I knew. I turned the knob. Mamá and Papi echoed each other's snore. One fat lump next to one skinny. I went to the skinny.

"Papi," I shook him.

He jumped up. "*Que-que?* Verdita?" He sniffed and rubbed his eyes.

Mamá rolled her belly to the side. "Faro?"

"I can't sleep," I said. I didn't want to tell them I was afraid of the Chupacabra, and I couldn't tell them about Carlos. "I don't feel good. I think I caught the mountain mist," I lied. Papi looked to Mamá. It was a bad lie, but I didn't have time to plan a good one.

"*Ay.*" Mamá shook her head, pushed over, and patted the space between her and Papi. "You want to sleep here?"

I hadn't climbed into bed with them for a long time. I wondered if I should, suddenly nervous that Papi would notice the lumps on my chest through my nightshirt, that he might feel the growing guilty apples in me. I crossed my arms and stood by the side of their bed, hugging myself against the cool of night.

Mamá opened the sheet. The warm, familiar smell of their bodies rose up. Not the Old Spice or the bottled roses of the day, but the night smell, like corn after it was shucked. I missed that. Carefully I climbed in, Mamá's belly like a pillow in my back. Her knees spooned me and my knees fit perfectly in the nook of Papi's side. The three of us lay like puzzle pieces, and I let myself remember what it was like to love them.

Mamá ran her hand down the line of my back and whisper-sang, "*Los pollitos dicen, pio, pio, pio . . . La gallina busca el maíz y el trigo les da la comida y les presta abrigo.*"

The Chupacabra seemed so unreal next to that moment. Our three breaths moved in and out together, protecting each other. I swam toward my dreams on the melody of Mamá, sleeping deep and soundless.

IN THE FUZZINESS of early morning, I was startled awake.

"Ow!" Mamá yelled, and sat up gripping her belly. Her knees jabbed me in the tailbone, and my knees did the same to Papi's side.

"Aw," he groaned. "Venusa? Watch out, Verdita." He pushed me to the side so he could reach Mamá.

"The baby kicked me. Feel."

Papi put his hand on her belly. "*Ay bendito!* It must be a boy. Strong."

They laughed. I sat alone on the edge of the bed, watching the light pattern the walls, my eyes adjusting. Then Mamá began to sing. Only this time, it wasn't to me.

"*Los pollitos dicen, pio, pio, pio.*"

She rubbed her belly and hummed. That was my song, not the baby's. It stole it from me, just like it stole Mamá and Papi. I left the bed. It was settled; they didn't love me anymore. They were having a boy. Just what Papi always wanted. What did they need me for except to shuck the corn and take the blame for everything? Carlos could do what he wanted to me; the Chupacabra could suck my blood. Either way, when they found me dead, *they'd* feel guilty.

"Verdita," Papi called.

My heart filled up warm. "Papi?" I said, hoping they might call me back, beg me to return.

"Do you want to feel the baby?" Mamá asked.

Papi waved his hand toward Mamá. "Come."

My fingers went cold and numb. "No."

I marched back to my room. The sheets were stretched across the tiled floor. I pulled them over my shoulders like a cape and dragged them to bed. The sun was rising. It lit up my room, exposing the corners for corners and the door for a door. There was no make-believe monster. No Carlos. Nothing. I closed my eyes and put the pillow over my head until I fell back to sleep. I dreamed that the Chupacabra grew inside of Mamá, making her white and drinking her blood until none was left, then it split her belly open, looking for me and Papi to feast on. I woke later to the sound of Omar and Blake dragging their suit-cases across the hall tiles. On the bed, white lines sliced my body to pieces where the bright daylight shone through the window slats.

*Chapter Eleven*

# The World Within, the World Beyond

MAMÁ'S BELLY GREW BIG IN THE HEAT OF MID-
summer. And the bigger it got, the thinner her
arms and legs became. She reminded me of
the pincushion she kept for mending shirts, a fat, brown
sand-sack with thin needles sticking out.

She stopped sleeping, unable to find a comfortable po-
sition, and complained that the baby kicked at her bones.
So she sat on the couch all day and all night, watching the
television and crocheting the blue and white blanket that
now rolled over the entire living room floor. Mamá said
the baby pushed on her bladder too, and sometimes she'd
wet herself in the middle of dinner or on the couch or
when she walked from the chicken coop to the house.
Because of that, she didn't go to town or even to church

anymore; and when people came over, she hid her enormous body in the bedroom until they left. She stopped having Señora Delgado and the prayer group visit. And when Titi Lola or Titi Ana came, she had me close the bedroom door and say she was sleeping. I was embarrassed for her. She didn't look or act like my mamá. Not the beautiful woman that I hated and loved. She barely spoke, and when she did, her voice was thin and small, like each word hurt. She had completely transformed.

Papi said I needed to help Mamá until the baby came. She was too sick to be alone while he worked the long farm hours and spent even longer ones at the *jíbaros* bar. But being nurse to Mamá was not my idea of fun. I ached to jump into another world and leave that one.

I searched Papi's study for something, anything, to take me away: worn Bibles and dusty journals, a handful of *National Geographics* with curled-up covers, notebooks filled with smudgy newspaper clippings, ripped books of poetry and ratty books of remedies, boxes of old photographs, distant relatives I'd heard of but had never met, my metal box with my birth certificate locked inside. On the top shelf, to the right of the dead roosters, was a dusty green book with gold lettering. It looked as old and untouched as the cocks. I climbed up and snatched it, being careful not to touch the stiff legs of the dead.

The cover read, *La Vida de Lazarillo de Tormes y de sus Fortunas y Adversidades*. The Life of Lazarillo de Tormes and of his Fortunes and Adversities. Swirling gold vines framed the edges. My stomach fluttered when I opened the cover and found a cartoon of a boy and a man on the first page. Someone had stamped the word PROHIBIDO over and over across the picture. I had discovered a world that someone wanted to keep a secret. Mamá and Papi? Or someone else?

The book was my gateway. Through it, I was free to leave our pink house and Mamá's constant groaning, to travel over the seas and walk the dusty roads of Spain. With Mamá's sickness and Papi always gone, I hid in the chicken coop collecting eggs and reading, excited by the adventures of young Lazarillo. I picked the day's vegetables and then sat in the dirt, eating tomatoes like apples, turning pages with seedy fingers. On the long trips to town for things Mamá needed, I carefully walked the winding roads with the book open in my fists, one ear listening for the whirring of cars and the other to the voice of Lazarillo. I was shocked and then afraid when I read that Lazarillo's wife and the Archpriest were lovers. I was on my way home and nearly dropped my basket of *pan de agua* and powdered milk. *Amantes.* Lovers. I finally had a word for it. Mamá and Papi were *amantes.* So were Carlos and Delia. And from Lazarillo, I realized that Blake's hand over my thigh wasn't enough to make us lovers or pregnant. It wasn't enough to make me a *puta*, either. By the time I turned the last page, I knew I could never go back to reading Dick and Jane. There was so much more in the world than tall buildings and automobiles.

I kept the book under my mattress, next to my journal, even after I'd finished. I couldn't put it back in the study. I was lonesome for Lazarillo's world, and hoped that by sleeping on it, I could go there in my dreams.

On my next trip to town, I stopped at the library and checked out an English book, *East of Eden*, because I once saw a picture of James Dean at the salon. He and Blake looked alike. I figured that book was the closest I could get to him and the States.

"VERDITA," MAMÁ CALLED on the afternoon I had just started *East of Eden*. I sat on the porch with a bowl of cut watermelon and a pillow propped behind my back, but my mind was walking the hills of California, U.S.A. I prayed Mamá would leave me alone. I was tired of her whining, tired of everything that had to do with the baby, and it wasn't even born yet.

I held my breath and listened to see if she would call again. She didn't.

Because of her belly, Mamá never left her room anymore, not even to lie on the couch and watch television. She was in bed all day, awake, with a cold cloth over her eyes, complaining that I was being too noisy or worrying that I didn't make the *arroz con habichuelas* correctly. She didn't like anyone near her. She said every touch was painful.

Later I put down my book and, still dreaming of

America, went to make sure Mamá hadn't wet herself, and to see if she wanted rice soup. That was all she could stomach.

"Are you hungry?" I asked. She gripped my hand and squeezed it hard.

"Señora Delgado," she whispered. "You know where she lives."

"Should I get Papi?" Something wasn't right. Her eyes were beady and ringed yellow.

"No. Just the midwife." She covered her face with the cloth.

Señora Delgado had delivered most everyone in the *barrio*. I wondered if the baby was coming. Teline said that when Pepito came, Titi Lola wet the bed and cried out for hours. Mamá's sheets reeked of urine and sweat, but she didn't cry. In fact, she barely breathed. Her belly loomed over, knotted and hot, and seemed to bury her alive.

I ran down the tarred main road, hugging the brush, cars whirring and swerving by, until I came to Señora's aqua house with white-painted iron on the windows and door. Pink and purple orchids climbed the fencing and smelled like candy. I caught my breath on the front stoop.

"Señora Delgado?"

Señora Delgado came to the mesh door and squinted. She was a large woman with strange violet eyes that matched her flowers. "Who's there?"

"Verdita Ortiz-Santiago," I said.

"Sí, Venusa's girl. I thought so, but my eyes—they're not so good as they used to be." She opened the door. "You like Florecitas? I have a bowl of them right here." She took my hand and pulled me into the living room.

"No, *gracias*, Señora. My mamá sent me."

"Her baby has another few weeks. What does she want?"

"She's sick. She told me to get you."

"Everyone feels sick at the end. Sick and tired of having a baby inside!" She laughed. "Tell her to drink some chamomile tea and suck on those ginger peels. If that doesn't work, tell her to put a lemon to her nose and smell it for ten minutes. And make sure she eats at least seven bananas a day. Okay? Here, take a Florecita for your walk home." She handed me a cookie with a hard, yellow icing rosette.

"But, Señora—" This was different. I didn't want the baby to come, rip right through Mamá, when I was alone. "She hasn't left the bed for weeks."

"Normal." She ushered me to the door.

"She barely eats. Her arms and legs are thin as bamboo!" I was desperate. I put my back to the door and held the latch so she couldn't reach. "Her eyes are yellow and she wets herself. The baby is killing her!"

The image of the Chupacabra bursting Mamá's belly seemed as real as the Florecita crumbled in my palm, as real as Lazarillo, as real as anything I believed in. I didn't want my dreams to come true—for it to feast on Mamá and then come after me. I wanted Señora there.

"*Ay bendito*. Relax, Verdita." She patted my arm. "Okay," she sighed, "I come." She pulled a shawl over her shoulders, and I released the latch.

WHEN SEÑORA DELGADO walked into our house, she took one sniff of the air and crossed herself.

"Here," she said, and pulled a gold bracelet with a coral stone off her wrist. "Put this on."

The stiffness of her words told me I shouldn't argue, so I did as she said and followed her back to the bedroom.

"Venusa?" Señora Delgado said, but Mamá didn't move. She flung the sheets off Mamá's body, exposing the giant belly, lumpy and mottled like a canker on the side of a tree. Mamá wore no panties. I looked away, ashamed for her, reminded of my own body in the creek and what she had told me about *putas*.

Señora Delgado palmed Mamá's foot and then rubbed it. "She's hot. It's the evil eye. I need wet cloths."

I threw every washcloth we had into the tub, ran the spigot, and scooped them up. At the edge of the bed, I stood with soggy arms and a puddle at my feet. Señora Delgado pushed up Mamá's chest, and for a moment I was sure Mamá was dead. Her eyes rolled back in her head showing only the yellow whites. I hugged the cloths to my chest; water dripped down my arms. I didn't want her to die.

She moved her arm to her belly. "It hurts," she moaned.

"Verdita, put them on her legs and over her stomach," Señora Delgado instructed.

I laid the wet cloths over Mamá. She tried to kick, but only managed to flinch against the cold.

"Get your papi," Señora Delgado said. "She needs to go to the hot springs in Coamo. I can't get her there. We need a man to lift her. Go!"

It was late in the day. Papi wasn't on the *finca* anymore. I knew where he was.

I dialed the number to the *jíbaros* bar. My heart pounded in my ears, temples, and forehead. It was my fault! God was answering my prayers, punishing Mamá and the baby. My stomach knotted. I hadn't come when she called me, and now she was dying. The phone rang four times before someone answered.

"Please, I need Señor Santiago. Faro Santiago!" Mamá began to scream. I dropped the phone. "Mamá!"

Señora Delgado rocked her and rubbed her belly. "Where's your papi?"

I couldn't answer. The phone dangled by the cord.

"Hello? Hello?" Papi's voice was so far away.

"Papi, Mamá is sick. God is punishing—"

Mamá howled.

"Verdita! What is it?"

"I prayed, and Mamá got sick, and the baby is killing her because it's a Chupacabra." My thoughts raced back and forth. The colors of the room blurred.

"Verdita," Papi said.

"Please, Papi! Help me!" I cradled the phone and hugged my head to my knees.

"I'm coming!"

"It's my fault," I whispered into the phone. But there was no one there to hear. The line was dead.

I sat on ground beside the bed, with my knees pulled up to my chest, singing "Los Pollitos" to myself while Mamá screamed. Señora Delgado rubbed her stomach with a washcloth until Papi came, then she covered her with the sheet.

"Venusa!" Sweat trickled down Papi's forehead and neck, and pooled in the dippy area below his throat.

"Faro, she needs to go to Coamo," explained Señora Delgado. "The mineral waters will help. She cannot have the baby yet. It is too early."

Papi wasn't listening. He wrapped a sheet around her and scooped her into his arms like the wet rags I carried.

"Verdita, come!" Papi commanded, and I followed behind. "We are going to the hospital in San Juan."

"But that is an hour away. She just needs—" Señora Delgado began.

"She needs a doctor."

Papi laid Mamá in the backseat of the jeep, and I climbed into the front, buckled my seat belt, and said prayers to the Virgin Mary card in the rearview mirror. I didn't need it to talk to God, but I wanted to see something holy.

As we pulled away, Señora Delgado stood in the front

yard, her limp shawl hanging over her arms bangled with gold *azabaches*. I hid mine from Papi. He'd be angry if he saw.


I SAT ALONE in the San Juan hospital waiting room, gray couches against gray walls along gray carpeting. I was drowning in gray. On the wall was a framed picture of Jesus, his chest torn open, his heart aflame. The single window looked out over concrete buildings. Green palm trees stuck through the street cracks like weeds. The room reminded me of one giant confessional booth. Only no priest was there to give me penance. I imagined Papi sat here while I was being born, and I wondered if he had felt the same way.

A nurse in a blue uniform with a white apron brought me a cup of apple juice. It was tangy and tasted nothing like the apples I ate at home.

"Your papi is with your mamá."

I knew that already. The nurse spoke in a singsong voice, like Bambi in the *cine*.

"She is very sick."

I knew that, too.

"I can get you anything you need. More juice?"

I shook my head. My cup was still half full. Too sweet. The nurse didn't say anything more, and I said nothing at all. I thought about *East of Eden* to keep from thinking about how I'd prayed for this. I tried to picture the mountains and valleys exactly as the book said. I figured California and Washington, D.C., probably looked the same. They were both in the States. I wondered what Blake and Omar were doing at that very moment. Eating dinner? Playing baseball? I missed them and felt lonelier having imagined them at all.

The sky turned orange, then purple-pink, and finally black. The colors smeared into one another, and I wished I could disappear into air and float around the world on the breeze. I prayed that I wouldn't be alone here anymore, that God would let Mamá live, that the baby wouldn't be a Chupacabra, but I still didn't want a boy.

When Mamá Juanita came through the waiting room doors, I couldn't move fast enough to reach her.

"I'm here, *nena*. I'm here," she said.

I buried my face in the smell of her cocoa-butter body and didn't hold back the twisted sounds that came from my throat. I wanted to explain what I'd done. I wanted to confess, but my mouth and tongue wouldn't fit together to make words. She rubbed my back until the sobs passed, and then led me out of the room.

We took a taxicab from the hospital to Mamá Juanita's. It was my first time in one, but I couldn't enjoy it, couldn't even bring myself to keep my eyes open. They batted between seeing and sleeping until I felt the softness of sheets skim over me, and I stopped fighting.

*Chapter Twelve*

# Adam, Eve, and the Fruit

I WOKE THE NEXT MORNING AND DIDN'T REMEMBER
where I was. Crocheted curtains hung in scalloped webs
along the open windows of the bedroom. The sun didn't
cut through the blinds in stripes like at home; instead, it
peeked through the holes in odd shapes that moved with
the wind. White rainbows danced on the blue-green walls,
like being underwater.

Mamá Juanita's house was different from mine; it felt
safe. I let myself forget to remember the day before, the
weeks before, even the year before. I pretended that the
room was deep beneath the sea in the castle of the Ocean
King, and I was his mermaid princess. But the pretending
didn't last. Sooner than I wanted, I remembered Mamá's
cries and the taste of apple juice. The coral stone from
Señora Delgado's bracelet tickled my wrist. I started to
take it off, but was afraid of what might happen if I did.

Mamá said that Señora Delgado was a woman who saw things—things that even the priests didn't see. The light flickered on the bedroom walls. I'd keep the *azabache* on a little longer.

Down the hall, Mamá Juanita spoke to someone. I threw back the covers and followed the sound. In the kitchen, Papi sat at the table.

"Papi!" I yelled. He turned, his eyes red and swollen. I'd never seen him cry.

"Is she—" My voice choked on itself.

"No, Verdita," Mamá Juanita said, and pulled me to her side.

I reached my hand out for Papi. I wanted him to say it, but he kept quiet.

"Your mamá is sick with an infection. The babies need to come out of her, but they are still too small."

"Babies?"

"She has twins inside her." Papi spoke low.

"Fraternal. Do you know what that means?" Mamá Juanita asked.

I didn't.

"You have a sister and a brother," she explained.

I didn't know any person who'd had more than one baby at a time. Cats and dogs and chickens, yes, but not people.

"I've got to go back. The operation starts at noon," said Papi.

"Operation?" I asked.

"The babies have the infection too. The doctors need to give them medicine. You understand?" asked Mamá Juanita.

I did. Mamá was sick. The babies were sick. The doctors would make them better. Papi ran a hand through his dark hair. With no pomade, it stuck up in different directions. It looked like mine. He left it like that, then rubbed his eyes.

"Here, take a little rice and beans." Mamá Juanita handed Papi a bowl covered with brown paper.

I found my sandals by the door, slipped them on, and went to Papi's side.

"I can carry the rice and beans." I reached out for them, but Papi didn't let go. Instead, he pulled away.

"No. You're staying."

"But I want to go."

He walked to the door. Mamá Juanita put her hands on my shoulders and tried to hold me in the kitchen, but I wriggled free and wrapped my arms around his waist.

"Papi, please!"

"Verdita, you are too young. Stay here with Mamá Juanita." He unclenched my arms.

I wasn't too young. I was nearly a *señorita*. I could help. "I'm carrying the rice." I grabbed the dish in his hands.

"Verdita, stop it!" Papi yelled.

The rice and beans teetered and nearly fell over, but I couldn't stop.

"Let go!"

The more he pushed, the tighter I gripped. I'd hold on until he had no choice but to take me.

Then, in one swift movement, he lifted his hand and slapped me across the jaw. The bones in my ears drummed, my teeth rattled, even my eyeballs seemed to click in their sockets. I let go and held my cheek, listening to the music in my head. It had been some time since Papi had lifted his hand, and even longer since he'd actually hit me. A fire built behind my eyes and lit my tongue.

"I wish you'd all die. I'm better off alone!" I covered my mouth; my lips burned.

I ran to the underwater bedroom and locked myself inside. Papi left a few minutes later. From the lacy window, I peeked out the holes to watch the jeep move down the street and out of sight.

Mamá Juanita didn't come in. I waited for her. First I sat on the floor with crossed arms, my face still warm from the slap. I heard her go by a few times, but she never tried to open the door. I wanted her to come and tell me how awful it was for Papi to hit me—how she understood. But she didn't. So I pretended to sleep. But that got old and the sheets made me sweat. I walked around the room a few times, but there was nothing to do, and I couldn't pretend away the sting on my cheek.

Soon I started to think—about the babies, about Mamá's sickness, about the operation. I wished I hadn't said what I had. I just wanted us to be together.

The door creaked when I opened it. The pads of my feet smacked the tiled floor, so I walked on tiptoes.

"Are you better?" Mamá Juanita asked.

I couldn't see her. "*Sí*," I whispered, and rounded the corner.

She sat at the kitchen table with a bowl of oranges and a book of prayers. "*Bueno*. Do you want an orange?" she asked.

An orange sat white and bare on a plate; its skin curled in one loopty loop peel beside it. Papi could do that too—peel an orange in a long, bright ribbon. He'd learned from her.

I took a seat. Mamá Juanita rolled a new orange back and forth between her palms. Then, with a small kitchen knife, she skinned it white. The orange twirl fell onto the plate with the other skin, like a festival streamer. She cut a triangle in the top, scooped out the stem, and handed it to me.

I sucked the clean, sweet juice until the orange was squashed and empty. Mamá Juanita handed me a napkin, but I didn't use it. I wanted the bright smell of oranges to stay on my fingers, and I was hungry for more.

"Can I have another?" I asked.

"*Sí*. Here. You can do it." She handed me the knife and another orange.

"I don't know how. I'll mess it up."

"So what if you do?" She continued to read the book of prayers.

I sat for a moment, the orange in my left hand, the blade in my right. My stomach kicked again. I rolled the orange, then stuck the knife tip into the stem. It was thicker than I thought, and my hands shook from trying to keep it just below the skin, trying to make the perfect curl, trying to keep from slicing my fingers.

"Look." I smiled up at Mamá Juanita. I was halfway around, the peel curling over my thumb.

"You're a natural," she said.

I pulled the knife along confidently, holding it close, eyeing every bumpy pore. Then, suddenly, the blade slipped through the white, piercing the fruit inside. Juice squirted into my eyes and dribbled down my cheeks. It burned. My eyes watered. Rubbing made it worse, and soon I was crying. I hadn't meant to, but my eyes did it on their own, even when I tried to make them stop. And then I stopped trying. I let the tears come, pour out, wash away the sting and cool my cheeks.

Mamá Juanita handed over another napkin, and I used it to wipe my face clean.

"Try again." She passed me a third orange. "Sometimes you have to make mistakes to find the right way. That's why God put so many oranges on one tree."

"What's the secret?" I asked.

"The secret is there's no secret. *Papá Dios* gave each person his own hand. You have to find your own way of doing it."

I rolled the orange back and forth until it was soft and juicy.

"Your papi must have gone through two dozen oranges before he found his way of peeling," Mamá Juanita said. "And you nearly got it on your first try."

I cupped it in my palms. Smelled it. Ran my tongue over the rippled skin and thought of Papi sitting beside Mamá Juanita with two dozen half-peeled oranges.

"Mamá Juanita, I'm sorry. I didn't mean what I said." I stuck the tip of the knife just under the stem and cut between the skin and flesh.

"I know," she said. "We all say things we don't mean. Everything will be okay. God is with them."

I held the blade steady and turned the orange. The peel twisted around my hand and hung in a limp curlicue over my wrist. It reminded me of the ponytail curls Mamá used to pomade my hair into when I was little. I missed the feel of her fingers smoothing the rough kinks on my head. Rounding the bottom, I sliced it clean, then held up the white fruit and the orange peel. I wished Papi and Mamá were there to see it.

"Very good, Verdita!" said Mamá Juanita. She buttered two pieces of bread for breakfast, and I skinned four more oranges. I ate it all, hungrier than I had ever been, it seemed.

Afterwards, Mamá Juanita put down her book of prayers. "What do you say we go to El Morro?"

I had only ever passed by the fortress. Papi always said he would take me when we had time to spare, but we never had it.

"You would like that. And besides," she sighed, "we need something to take our minds off things, *sí?*"

I couldn't agree more.

THE ENTRANCE TO El Morro stood at the end of a long, green field on the edge of a cliff. Mamá Juanita and I walked past the spot where we'd lain in December. I wished I could go back to that moment. Now there were no children flying kites, only a group of shirtless older boys chasing a soccer ball from left to right. The sun was out, but the sun was always out in San Juan. I couldn't remember a time when the city wasn't outlined in gold.

We walked the dirt roadway toward the entrance, passing a family speaking a language I'd never heard before—not English or Spanish. Maybe French. Or Chinese. I wondered how many different languages were in the world. I only knew two, but I wanted to learn at least five.

"Where are they from?" I asked Mamá Juanita.

"I don't know. Sounds German or Russian," she said, and took my hand so we could pass quickly.

Russia was a big red chunk of land on Señora Alonzo's map—a hundred times bigger than Puerto Rico, bigger than the United States. Russia was communist like Cuba.

Ahead on the path was a tour group guided by a man wearing a white, buttoned-up shirt tucked into a pair of teal shorts with matching sneakers.

"This is the largest Spanish fort in the Caribbean, taking over two hundred years to complete," the guide said in English.

"Mamá Juanita, look—Americans?" I whispered.

"*Sí*. We have lots of them here."

In the group was a blond girl who looked my age. She watched me and I watched her. She had a round face and bowed lips and skin the color of coconut milk. I wondered if her name was Jane. The group stopped to take photos while we went on. I wished I was part of their group, wished I could stop and talk to Jane—be her friend. But she was a stranger to me, and I to her.

Inside, we walked the stone steps of El Morro alongside other tourists. On the highest lookout, a plaque read that gunmen had kept watch for U.S. ships during the Spanish-American war on that spot. Farther down, along the fortress wall, was Fort San Cristobal. Its black cannons still aimed toward the sea. I wondered if they kept them there waiting for the next to come and try to claim our beaches. Across the horizon, a cruise ship with colorful flags sailed by the weapon line.

A round lookout hole in an empty turret framed the port of San Juan. Through it were white ships strung with glittering lights and flags. Antlike men and women walked the brown decks and in and out of the bridged walkways reaching from ship to land. Names like *Bianca C* and *Empress of Canada* were printed on the sides of the ships.

"Look at those boats!" I said to Mamá Juanita.

"Rich Americans and English," she replied. "Your Titi Carmen lives in Miami, you know, and they have many of these there. People sailing all over the world on holiday."

"Where are they going?" I asked.

"Nowhere. They just want to get away from where they were."

A woman leaned against the top deck railing of the *Empress of Canada*. I wondered what her story was.

"I bet they're happy in between places," I said to Mamá Juanita. "Not worried about what they left or where they're going."

"*Sí*, I guess so." Mamá Juanita pulled a pink clamshell compact from her purse and fluffed her hair. "But me— I like to get where I'm going. I'd get bored sailing in a big circle. Where have you gone? Nowhere. You end up in the same place you started and what good is that? I like to know for certain where I am." She put the compact back in her purse when a Chinese family, in matching purple T-shirts, stopped nearby.

I watched the boats through the cannon hole. It was like a spyglass to a secret world. So clear and yet so far. I'd be happy on that ship. I just knew it.

"*Scusi?*" said a man in a wide-brimmed straw hat and mango-colored pants.

"No, no, Bob, honey, for God's sake, that's Italian. They speak Spanish. Espanole," said a woman with cropped brown hair and big white sunglasses. She looked like a bumblebee.

"Oh yes. Okay. Umm, *Por favor, un foto?*" Bob asked and then smiled as wide as his hat.

They both had small lips and strong jaws. Blond stubble grew in patches on Bob's cheeks, but his face didn't look dirty and rough, like Papi's when he didn't shave. It looked fuzzy, like the face of a stuffed animal. The woman was pink-cheeked and pink-lipped and stood with her head up, like a movie actress. They were bright and friendly.

"We speak English," I said. Eager to use all the words I knew. "Are you Americans?"

"Yes. We're from Connecticut. On our honeymoon," Bob replied, and kissed the top of his wife's head.

"Congratulations," said Mamá Juanita.

"Congratulations," I said too.

"Thank you." The woman smiled up at Bob, then stuck out her hand. "I'm Jill." I took it and shook. It was small and soft, and I knew without a doubt that she'd never cracked a coconut or peeled a plantain or shucked corn in her whole life. Her fingers were smooth as water, and I worried that she could feel the calluses on my palm.

"Beautiful island you got here." She reached out to Mamá Juanita next. "Just gorgeous." They shook, and Mamá Juanita smiled and shrugged as if Jill had just complimented *her.*

"I'm Juana, and this is Maria Flores," said Mamá Juanita.

She used our formal names with the Americans. They were strangers. But I wanted them to know the real me—Verdita.

"You can call me Verdita. It's what everybody does." Mamá Juanita shot me a look.

"Nice to meet you, Verdita," said Bob.

My name sounded different when he said it. The *Ver* was strong and clear and didn't roll together with the *dita*.

Bob handed Mamá Juanita his Minolta. We didn't own a camera, but I'd seen pictures of them in magazines and on television. I was jealous that Mamá Juanita got to use it. She looked through the back while Bob and Jill posed—arms wrapped around each other, big smiles. We only had one photograph of Mamá and Papi. Their wedding day. They didn't have a honeymoon. Papi said that Puerto Ricans didn't take honeymoons because the island was already paradise and every day was a celebration. I figured that was true; why else would people like Jill and Bob come?

Mamá Juanita pushed a button and the camera made a small click. I'd expected more.

"Nice camera. My daughter has one like this. She lives in Miami," Mamá Juanita handed it back to them.

"That's where we boarded. Pretty—Miami," said Bob.

It was all happening so fast. We were talking to them, meeting them. I knew their names. Bob and Jill. Jill and

Bob. Dick and Jane. Of course they were Americans. With those smiles and happy lives, what else could they be?

"Hey, any chance you could tell us a good joint to eat? We're dying to try some of the food here. All we get on the ship is pork chops, steak, and salmon. I'm sick of it." Bob laughed. It sounded more like a cough, but I could tell by his smile and the way his eyes welled that it was a laugh.

I wondered how anybody could get sick of pork chops, steak, or salmon. It sounded pretty good to me. I'd only had bread and oranges for breakfast. I bet all Americans ate pork chops, steak, and salmon—plates and plates of it. I'd never had pork chops, steak, or salmon, but I'd had plenty of chicken.

"Try *arroz con pollo*—rice with chicken. It's good," I said and tried to make my smile as wide as theirs.

"Rice and chicken?" said Bob.

Mamá Juanita gave them directions to La Bombonera, an old restaurant on Calle San Justo. The owner's wife played bingo with her on Monday nights.

"Great. Nice meeting you both. If you're ever in Hartford, Connecticut, look us up. Milford. Bob and Jill. We'll take you out for some of the best pizza you ever tasted," Bob said.

I didn't know what pea-sa was, but I nodded like I did. It sounded like a bean dish, pigeon peas, I figured.

They walked hand in hand out the entrance and across the long path. I wanted to go to Connecticut to visit them.

I wanted to eat pea-sa, pork chops, steak, and salmon. I wanted to see my *titis* and *tíos,* and Omar and Blake in Washington, D.C. I didn't want to be stuck on this island with Chupacabras and evil spirits and sickness. I wanted to go to the United States where everybody smiled and was happy.

WE WENT TO the hospital that night and sat in the gray waiting room once again. Papi stood across from us, staring out the window at the black sky. We didn't talk about what had happened at Mamá Juanita's. But I couldn't be mad at Papi for long. Mamá, yes, but Papi was different. Our spirits were connected. He knew I was sorry, and I knew he felt bad for hitting me. I wanted to forget it had ever happened, so I thought about the white sunglasses on Jill, the straw hat on Bob. I wondered if they liked the *arroz con pollo* as much as I did.

They operated on Mamá and took out a boy, a girl, and Mamá's womb. A doctor in a long white coat came out. He said big words like *complication* and *hysterectomy* and *chorioamnionitis.* Words I had never heard in my life. Words much bigger than *automobile.* The only thing I knew for sure was that Mamá was okay, sleeping finally.

"Mr. Santiago, if you'd like to spend some time with your daughter, I suggest you do it now," the doctor said.

I turned to Papi. I was right there.

"The baby daughter," Mamá Juanita whispered.

Not me. I was almost a *señorita*.

Papi followed the doctor back, and an hour later, the nurse who'd given me apple juice told us that the girl had died. It seemed so far away, so dreamlike. I couldn't cry. I hadn't known her. Mamá Juanita crossed herself, and we said a prayer for her spirit. I imagined her swimming to heaven, her wavy black hair trailing behind; her light eyes shining through the night like a glow fish.

Papi returned soon after and sat beside me.

"You have a brother." He sighed and wrapped his arm around my shoulder. I leaned into him. His shirt was warm and damp and smelled sour-sweet, like the Borinqueneer uniform.

"I'm sorry, Papi," I whispered.

Papi nodded and kissed my forehead.

"How is the boy?" asked Mamá Juanita.

"Fine. The nurses have him," explained Papi.

"And Venusa?"

Papi sighed again. The breath moved through his throat, his chest, his lungs. It echoed against his bones.

"She cannot—" He sipped in air, but it seemed to get stuck in the knobby part of his neck. "No more children."

"You have a boy and a girl, Faro. An Adam and an Eve. Be thankful." Mamá Juanita pulled rosary beads from her purse and bowed her head.

*Chapter Thirteen*

# Naranja

T HEY NAMED THE BABY JUAN AFTER PAPI AND MY *abuelo*. Papi put me in charge of holding the birth certificate. I read it over and over.

> CERTIFICATE OF BIRTH: *Juan Ortiz-Santiago. Boy.*
> *August 2, 1962. San Juan, Puerto Rico.*
> FATHER: *Juan Santiago.* OCCUPATION: *farmer.*
> MOTHER: *Monaique Santiago de Ortiz.*
> OCCUPATION: *none.*

The nurse had a fair hand in printing. She wrote in loopy letters and dotted her *i*'s in circles, not black holes, making the words look like they had misplaced eyeballs. All in all, it was a nice certificate.

Mamá and the baby spent three days in the hospital before they were released. I wasn't allowed to see them.

Papi said they were still sick and needed rest. So I stayed at Mamá Juanita's.

When I finally saw Mamá again, a nurse wheeled her out of the hospital entrance, and she looked nothing like she had before. Her stomach was gone; her hair was pulled back in a lopsided bun, and her face was pale except for the dark lines of her eyebrows. She barely spoke, even when I kissed her cheeks and hands to let her know I never wanted her to leave for good.

"Come meet your brother," Papi said. He held Juan in his arms, wrapped in a thin, blue hospital blanket.

I stepped away, worried that he knew all the wrong I'd wished him before he was born. Papi leaned in close and peeled back the blanket. A little orange face squinted against the light, pursed his lips, and fell back to sleep.

"He's a different color from us," I said.

"It's called jaundice," Papi explained. "It will pass."

Papi pulled the blanket back over the baby's face and handed him to Mamá.

"No," Mamá grunted, and pulled herself into the front seat of the jeep. "Verdita can hold."

Papi nodded. "Can you?"

I'd never held a newborn baby before. "What if I hurt him?"

Papi smiled. "I don't think you'll hurt him."

I climbed in and buckled my seat belt. Papi handed me the bundle, and I cradled him the best I could, his head in the crook of my arm, his feet snuggled against my waist. He fit perfectly in my lap.

"*Naranja,*" I whispered. He smelled like dusted sugar. "I'm your sister, Verdita."

Papi started the jeep. "What did you call him?"

"*Naranja,*" I said. "'Cause he's orange."

"*Naranja,*" Papi repeated. "Like I said, Puerto Ricans are all colors of the rainbow," he laughed, and it felt good to hear it again. "What do you think, Venusa?"

Mamá leaned against the side of the window without answering.

"I think it's a good nickname," he said.

On the way home from the hospital, we passed a group of people as big as the crowd that had gathered to see President Kennedy. For a split second I wondered if he had returned without my knowledge, but then I saw a man holding a poster with a black X through the American flag. He was shouting something with fist raised in the air. The man next to him held a sign that read: *Movimiento Pro-Independencia.* The crowd began to chant "MPI," and pounded the air to a furious cadence.

Naranja slept in my arms, his tiny breath moving in and out, his heart thumping warm and steady. I held him close as we passed the protesters, shielding him from their voices and angry glares.

"Papi, why are those people so mad?" I asked once the crowd was behind us.

"Politics." Papi shook his head. "By trying to make us a state, they think America is stealing Puerto Rico—our traditions, our people. So they fight for independence. Many Puerto Ricans believe you must be hot or cold. American or Boricuan. To be lukewarm is worse than death," he explained.

I knew that was in the Bible, so it had to be true. "What are we?" I asked.

Papi sucked his teeth. "We are what we are," he said, and I could tell by the tone of his voice that that was enough. I didn't dare ask more, even though I was more confused than ever, and ashamed of my longings to be both.

When we got home, Naranja woke but didn't cry, even when I bumped his feet against the screen door. Mamá went straight into her room and locked the door.

"She is still recovering," Papi explained. "We'll put him in the living room for now."

Papi pulled my old cradle from the storage closet while I rocked Naranja on the couch. He made funny noises. Gurgles and hiccups and farts. They made me laugh, and when I did he yawned and stretched and made more noises, and I laughed some more. He was good as far as babies went, as far as boys went, too. And I started to love him. I hadn't meant to. Each time he giggled or farted or blew a spit bubble, one of my fears about having a baby brother popped open and flew off on the night breeze. A wild dog howled somewhere in the distance, and I pulled

Naranja close to my chest. Slipping the gold *azabache* off my wrist, I slid it onto his, and pushed it up until it fit the upper part of his arm. Papi wouldn't mind; *azabaches* were meant for babies. Everyone in Puerto Rico put them on newborns to keep jealous spirits from taking them back to heaven.

In the middle of the living room, we set up the cradle, a basket on stilts padded with Mamá's blue and white blanket that spilled over the edges and touched the floor. Naranja looked like the baby Jesus in the *Navidad* scene. I pulled a chair close to him and touched his orange cheeks and chubby fingers. The tiny knuckles of his fingers reminded me of fresh corn kernels.

Over the next few days he slept a lot. And when he wasn't sleeping, he ate formula, pooped, and cried. But he only cried when he wanted to eat or after he pooped, and I wished he could just tell us which one instead of wailing so loud that he woke the chickens. I wondered when he would learn to talk, and if he would speak English or Spanish. Or maybe he'd speak some other language—Russian or Chinese. Maybe God had accidentally given us a Chinese baby. I'd have to learn Chinese to talk to him, and Mamá and Papi wouldn't understand. It would be our own secret language.

Mamá stayed in bed, only rising to use the bathroom. She ate a jar of peanut butter a day. The empty ones lined the side of the mattress; a full one sat on the bedside table, uncapped, with a spoon stuck in the middle like a grave marker. I brought her a loaf of *pan de agua* in the mornings and picked up its empty paper sleeve at night. Mamá lived the same life as Naranja: sleeping, eating, and crying.

Papi tried to get her to breast-feed Naranja, but she was still sick with the infection and didn't want to give it to "the boy." I explained to her his nickname, but by then the jaundice had faded. She took one look at him and said she didn't understand.

Almost a week went by and Mamá didn't get better, so Papi stopped by town and bought aspirin and peanut butter for Mamá, gin for himself, a sack of rice, Palmolive soap, and seven cans of Similac. I learned to fix the powdered formula. It was just like the Klim that Mamá used to give me. Each morning I made us milk for breakfast, adding a little peanut butter to mine. Afterwards, it was time to burp and, an hour later, to diaper. Every day was the same. We moved the cradle into my room so Mamá could get well. Naranja's cries made her breasts wet; it was best that he slept where she couldn't hear him.

I forgot about books, my journal, and the States, everything outside of the house, everything outside of Mamá, Papi, and Naranja. It was my penance. I did the cooking and the cleaning and the laundry, but none of it very well. All the clothes were dingy. I scrubbed diapers with Palmolive, but they turned yellow no matter what, and my arms couldn't reach the tops of the windows, so they stayed dirty. My *mixtas* tasted too salty, too soupy, but Papi ate them anyway, or at least he did at first. He stopped coming home for dinner after a while, and spent his nights at the *jíbaros* bar. Sometimes he didn't come home at all. When he did, he slept on the couch, and in the mornings I found him with pockets full of money and copper on his breath. I shook him hard to wake him and made *café con leche* the way Mamá did. Sometimes he drank it, sometimes he didn't. We sat at the breakfast table: Naranja and I with our milk, Papi with his *café*. Then he'd leave for work. We didn't talk.

Mamá stayed in her room with the door locked. I'd put my ear to the door and listen to her saying the rosary; the sound of her voice hummed through the wood, slow and steady. I couldn't stop wondering if she blamed me for everything that had happened. I blamed myself and wondered if God had cursed the baby girl and Mamá on account of my prayers, my wishes. I was sorry for hating her.

Papi said that Mamá named the baby girl, but never spoke her name. I called her Angela, because that was how I remembered her on the night she died.

ON FRIDAY OF that week, I was pulling dingy rags off the back laundry line when the loud clatter of women's voices interrupted.

"Venusa! Verdita!" Titi Lola called.

I left the clothes dangling by their pins. Papi was already at work; Mamá was locked in her room, and Naranja slept after his morning formula.

Titi Lola rapped on the screen door and called, "Any, one home?" With her were half a dozen women from town, including Delia, Titi Ana, Señora Delgado, and two women from the prayer group.

"*Sí*, we're here, Titi." I unlatched the front door.

"*Ay*, Verdita. How's my blond/ay bombshell?" My hair had almost grown out by then, frosted only at the tips. She kissed my cheeks. The others trailed in and did the same.

"It's been almost two weeks and no invitation to meet the new *bebito*, so we thought we'd come see for ourselves." Titi Lola scanned the dirty dishes in the sink, the mound of unfolded laundry on the couch, the empty Similac tins, and the half/washed windows. Her gaze settled on me, and I hoped I didn't look as unclean as I felt. She cocked her head and pursed her lips. "Hmm…" She waved to Delia, who carried two brown paper bags splotched with grease. "We brought food."

"Fried chicken," said Delia. She put the bags on the table, exposing her belly bump; it was not nearly as big as Mamá's had been.

The smell of chicken filled the air. I hadn't eaten any in months. I wondered if there was a cockfight the night before, if Papi had seen it while playing cards. Was this the losing rooster, bloodied and broken into oily pieces? I thought of the limp hen in Mamá's hands, moving its wings, swimming through the air like Angela toward heaven. My stomach knotted, but my mouth watered.

"The baby is in there?" Señora Delgado asked, eyeing the locked bedroom door.

"No," I said. My shirt was damp from the laundry and hugged tight to my body. I crossed my arms over my chest to hide the curves. "He sleeps in my room."

"Your mamá?" Señora Delgado started toward the door before I answered. Titi Ana and the prayer women followed.

"She's still sick. She doesn't come out, but I bring her food and change her sheets and check on her all the time," I explained.

"It's okay. We're here now." Titi Lola ran a hand over my head. "Delia, give Verdita something to eat."

Delia pulled fried chicken pieces from the bag and motioned with her head for me to eat. I couldn't.

"Venusa, open the door. It's me, Lola." Titi's voice was soft and low. She spoke to the crack of the doorframe.

"We can help," said Señora Delgado.

No answer.

"We understand, *querida*. Please," said Titi Lola.

Titi Ana began to hum, a soft monotone note that soon changed pitch with each woman's added voice. Slowly their sounds made words, and they sang:

*We shall overcome our pain, strong hearts and souls united.*
*We shall overcome to tell our stories bravely,*
*Our love defying sorrow's gain.*

The door remained closed. The women gathered before it.

*We'll sing of wounds healed by divine embrace.*
*We'll sing of loss restored by grace.*

I'd heard the prayer hymn before, at church, but never in the soft soprano of all women. It was different then, changed by them into a kind of magic.

They sang, voices full and high:

*We'll share our hearts with those who weep alone,*
*Chant songs of joy and courage to face the coming morn.*
*We'll celebrate the resurrection story,*
*And join our circle of love reborn.*

Delia put her hand over mine. The same hand that had slapped Teline beneath the mango tree. It wasn't as rough as I'd imagined. I left my hand beneath hers and blinked away the tears. Nothing was like I'd imagined.

The hymn ended, but I could still hear the music vibrating on the terra-cotta. Then the bedroom door opened. Mamá's ghostly face appeared. Tears streaked her cheeks and stained the front of her cotton nightgown. Titi Lola put her arms around her, and the group silently slipped into the room. They left the door open. Cracked, just a sliver. I could see the movement within.

"She'll be okay," said Delia.

Her dark eyes reflected my face and body, like a shadowy mirror, and I wasn't afraid of her and Carlos anymore. She'd loved and been loved. A baby was not a punishment. I understood that now.

"Where is your brother?" she asked.

"In my room." I led Delia there.

Inside the crib, he slept, his chest moving up and down, his lips puckered soft.

"We nicknamed him Naranja," I told Delia.

She cocked her head, like Titi Lola had earlier.

"He was born orange." I ran a finger over his tiny corn knuckles. "Orange like a new sun. I think his twin sister is the moon. She let him rise, but it meant she couldn't stay."

I hadn't thought about his story before that moment, but it came out as if I had told it a hundred times.

"Delia?" Titi Lola called.

We left Naranja and went to Mamá's room. Inside, the women sat around her on the bed.

"Bring me a basin of warm water, please," Titi instructed.

I helped Delia fill a bowl with heated water from the stove. We took it into the room, where the women unclothed Mamá. I didn't look away from her nakedness. It no longer shamed me. They wrapped a fresh sheet around her and stripped the bed of the dirty ones. We put the bowl on the floor, and leaning her back over the side of the mattress, the women silently washed her hair. The water trickled and splashed onto the floor. Titi Ana toweled the ground on hands and knees. After the suds were rinsed clean, Señora

Delgado began to sing another hymn, and the rest joined. I didn't know the words, but hummed along and helped Titi Lola comb the kinks from Mamá's hair. It was soft and smelled fresh and sweet. I ran my fingers through the silky strands. I had missed her.

When Naranja awoke, I brought him to the bedside.

"Give him to your mamá," instructed Señora Delgado, and I did as she said.

It was the first time Mamá had held him since the hospital. Her arms trembled with his weight.

"He's a good baby, Venusa. A strong boy," Titi Ana said.

"Naranja," Mamá whispered to his head. He gurgled spit bubbles, reached for her hair, and tangled himself in its waves. She didn't pull away, just stared down at him, running her thumb over his cheek.

The women stayed all day, cleaning, eating, and talking. When Naranja began to cry for food, I went for the Similac, but Señora Delgado stopped me. Mamá sat on the living room couch with Naranja. She pulled up her shirt and pressed his lips to her breast. Naranja fidgeted, cried out for the bottle in my hand, sucked and cried, sucked and cried. On the third try, Mamá's milk came, and he ate peacefully.

"The real thing is always best. Only a mamá can give that," said Señora Delgado, eyeing the trash can full of Similac tins and an empty bottle of gin.

"When is your papi coming home?" she asked.

"He's at work. And sometimes he stops by the *jíbaros* bar—for dinner and politics."

Titi Lola eyed Titi Ana and cleared her throat. Señora Delgado crossed herself, then took out the trash.

The women left late, but Papi still wasn't home. Mamá slept with Naranja in her bed. I missed his steady breathing in my room, but was too tired to think about it for long. My head was heavy, my eyelids too, so I lay down on the pillow and closed my eyes. I hadn't slept a full night since before Naranja was born, and I missed my dreams, even if they were only of quiet darkness.

In the morning I awoke to the smell of *funche* and *café con leche*. Mamá was not in the kitchen, though. I went to her room. It smelled clean, like the ocean. The windows were open, the bed made. The hump where Mamá's body had been for so long was smooth, the sheets drawn taut. She came out from the closet in a yellow dress, one of the salsa dresses that I never saw her wear. She'd pinned her hair up along her temples, long and wavy in the back, painted rouge on her cheeks and lips, and even curled her eyelashes. She looked beautiful. My stomach fluttered. Mamá!

"Are you hungry, *nena?*" she asked.

I went to her and wrapped my arms around.

At the breakfast table, she ladled sweetened cornmeal into my bowl and sat beside me, breast-feeding. "It's good?" she asked after I took a bite.

I nodded. Mamá smiled. I wanted to say so much. To tell her how sorry I was for everything, that I loved my baby brother, and that Papi would come home soon. He always did. He was just trying to forget the sad parts of Puerto Rico.

"I'm sorry," Mamá said before I could. "It wasn't fair to leave you alone."

I let my spoon sink into the buttery mush.

"Thank you, Verdita. You did a good job taking care of him."

I tried to lift my spoon, but it was caught, suctioned beneath. I couldn't look her in the eyes, afraid that she'd see everything I'd done to hurt her, so I stared at the bumpy grits of corn.

"I always dreamed of having children." She sighed. "After you were born, your papi and I tried for many years to give you brothers and sisters, but it was not God's will. Then one day I felt another baby growing inside me, and I knew that I was called to be a mother of more. I imagined the faces of all the children I would have. I began to name them." She rubbed the corner of her eye, then continued. "So when the doctors told me I could no longer carry a child, I thought my life was over. I thought your papi didn't need me—that you and Naranja didn't need me. I was wrong."

She reached across the table. I let go of my heavy spoon.

"Tell me, Verdita, what do you dream of?"

I dreamed of Papi's rainbow beach.

Naranja slept at Mamá's breast. Milk wet on his lips.

This was my chance. But I remembered the MPI men with their angry faces and hateful signs. My palms sweated; a chill ran down my spine. Was I hot or cold?

"I'd like to go to the United States," I said.

"The United States?" Mamá's eyes shifted out the front window framing Puerto Rico's mountains. "*Sí,*" she said.

She touched my head, smoothed a kinky curl. "I can still remember holding you like this." She rocked Naranja. "Now look. My little girl is a grown beauty."

I smiled, hopeful that Papi would agree.

Just after Mamá washed the pot and dumped the cold *café con leche* down the sink, Papi came through the front door in a stained *guayabera*, his face shiny with sweat, his eyes blistered red like a Chupacabra's.

"Verdita, take care of Naranja," Mamá said, and led Papi to the bedroom. She closed the door behind them. I held Naranja against my chest, his head lying on my shoulder, his face looking up into mine, asking questions I couldn't answer.

"It'll be okay," I told him.

Naranja blinked hard at my words and breath on his face.

Their voices carried through the walls, Papi's slurred, Mamá's steady. She said his name over and over.

Naranja's heart beat fast. I could feel it through my shirt. Mine did too. I took him out onto the porch.

"*Los pollitos dicen, pio, pio, pio,*" I sang. In the distance, over the green mountains and valleys, the ocean crested here and there in foamy white. On the other side of that sea sprung from a pumpkin was the United States and the rainbow beach, Omar and Blake, Jill and Bob. I wanted to visit Hartford, Connecticut, U.S.A., and bring Jill and Bob sesame seed bars. The three of us could sit on their porch, crunching on candy, wearing straw hats, and singing "The Star-Spangled Banner."

MAMÁ MADE *ARROZ mixto* for dinner that night, and I was sure it had never tasted so good. Papi came out of his room, washed and shaved, and pomaded smooth. His eyes were still ringed with red, but not nearly the bloodshot from earlier.

He sat at the head of the table. Mamá put a plate of *mixta* before him and took a seat, holding Naranja. Papi prayed over our food. A short prayer, his voice raspy and low.

When he finished, he turned to me. "Verdita, your mamá and I have spoken and she tells me you want to go to the United States. Is this true?"

I dropped my fork on my plate.

"*Sí,* Papi," I whispered.

"You can visit Tío Orlando, if that's what you want." He eyed Mamá, then looked down at his pile of red rice. "We'll make plans. You wouldn't be in America long."

"A few weeks," said Mamá.

Papi rubbed his brow, then looked up and our eyes met.

My thoughts swelled, and I was sure my brain would pop and seep out my ears, nose, and mouth. But it didn't. In fact, nothing came out except, "Papi! Mamá!"

I kissed their cheeks and danced around the table, even though they barely moved, barely smiled, barely ate. I was grateful and feasted until my belly was full, until every speck of chicken, every grain of rice, and every smear of oil was licked clean.

Later I lay in bed listening to coquis chirp, wondering if it was all true. Would they really let me go? My finger-tips tingled, and no matter how I fixed my pillow, I couldn't sleep.

It would be hard to leave them. And what if I started to forget things while I was away? Like how to speak Span-ish or how to cook *arroz mixta*, or the taste of fresh co-conut milk, the smell of banana leaves, the sound of coquis. What if I forgot Puerto Rico, like Omar? What if America stole Puerto Rico from me like the protesters said? And all at once my excitement changed. The butterflies in my stomach grew stone wings and batted against my rib cage, thumping and bruising my bones.

*Chapter Fourteen*

# Arriving in Between

Iɴ Nᴏᴠᴇᴍʙᴇʀ, Mᴀᴍᴀ́ Jᴜᴀɴɪᴛᴀ ᴜsᴜᴀʟʟʏ ᴡᴇɴᴛ ᴛᴏ visit Tío Orlando and my *titis* for the American Thanksgiving; but that year she decided to stay in Puerto Rico with Mamá, Papi, and Naranja. She gave her plane ticket to me.

On the day of my flight from San Juan, she kissed my forehead, blessed me, and told me to bring a coat because D.C. was like an icebox in the winter. I remembered Omar's story about the man who froze in front of the White House; but all my good dresses and white pumps were packed in a daisy-print suitcase, so Mamá Juanita gave me her green polka-dot sweater, five sizes too big. Papi pulled my suitcase from the jeep while I said good-bye to Mamá and Naranja.

"I bless you in the name of the Father, and the Son,

and the Holy Spirit." Mamá kissed my cheeks, forehead, and chin.

I laid my face against the white of her neck. "Thank you, Mamá."

"The next time I see you, you'll be a *señorita*. I'm certain." Her voice wobbled. She cleared her throat to steady it. "Don't change too much while you're gone, okay?"

I nodded, but didn't dare promise. Truth was, I hoped I came back changed. More American, for sure.

She handed Naranja to me so I could say good-bye.

"It's only a little while," I whispered. I didn't want him to think I'd forget him. Life had been good since he came. I'd been wrong to hate him, and was glad God didn't grant me my prayers. "Our spirits can meet on the rainbow dream beach every night." I kissed his head, sprouted with dark curlicues like my own. They'd grown so fast over the past four months. He grabbed my finger and held tight. I didn't want him to let go.

"Verdita, these planes don't wait for no one," Papi said. He, alone, was taking me to my boarding gate. Since Mamá got better, we hadn't really talked like we used to. He and I were different now.

"God bless you," Mamá Juanita said, putting her hand on my cheek one last time. The smell of cocoa butter lingered.

A smiling woman in a short blue dress took my suitcase, put a tag on the handle, and gave me back another tag. They were like puzzle pieces, she said. The two fit together so that if somebody else had a daisy-printed suitcase, I would know which was mine. My puzzle piece fit only my luggage.

"Don't lose that ticket," said Papi. "Keep it someplace safe and don't let it fall out." I pulled my gardenia journal from my bag and slid the ticket between the pages of mag-azine pictures, scribbled thoughts, memories, and dreams. It was safest there.

"Do everything they tell you on the plane," he went on, "Fasten your seat belt, and if you have to go to the bathroom, ask one of the women to take you. *Don't* go by yourself. *Don't* talk to any strangers. And *don't* get up out of your seat unless it is an emergency. And remember to chew gum, otherwise your ears will hurt—you have gum?"

I nodded and showed him my box of Chiclets.

"Good—and always pray during the takeoff and the landing. Always."

We were at my gate, but I didn't want to go yet. We hadn't talked about any of the important stuff like the *jíbaros* bar and the dead roosters; what they named the baby girl; his secret for peeling oranges; how to keep from forgetting Puerto Rico and . . .

"Verdita . . ." Papi's voice trailed off raspy, like he'd swallowed burnt *chicharrones.* "Here." He pulled an extra-large sesame seed bar from his pocket, the size he only bought on birthdays and holidays. "I know how you like these. And you deserve it." He looked down at the candy stretched out to me.

I thought he wanted me to take it, so I tried. But he didn't let go. Instead, he leaned forward and kissed the point where my hair stopped and my face started.

"*Mi'ja*." He stayed close for a moment.

I didn't want him to ever pull away, but he did.

"When you arrive, Tío Orlando will be waiting for you. Look for him. Okay?"

"*Sí*," I said. My voice was small. I tried to make it bigger. "Papi—"

"You have everything."

"*Sí, pero Papi*—" I began.

"English, Verdita. People won't understand you. They'll take you as ignorant. You must show these Americans that you are a smart girl. A Boricua! So only English in the States. You can speak Spanish when you're with the family."

I didn't argue. There was too much I wanted to say, and not much time.

"Get out your ticket. Hurry now," Papi said. My hands shook. "Give it to the lady, and she'll show you to your seat." His body stiffened; his cheeks barely moved when he spoke, and his eyes stayed away from mine. I couldn't stand it.

"Papi." I forced my face against his chest and breathed in the Old Spice, the gardenias, the chickens and the corn, the Schlitzes and *mixtas*, the brown dirt and the green, green island. He smelled like home.

Papi leaned his cheek on my head. "Mamá and I will

be right here to pick you up when you come back. I promise I'll take good care of her and Naranja."

I nodded. There was no time for talk, so I took a last
breath and held the smell inside my lungs, let it soak into
my flesh and bones so I would always remember.

"*Te quiero,*" I said.

"*También,*" he whispered then pushed me through the
gate.

The attendant took my ticket and led me through the
boarding tunnel. I didn't look back at Papi. I didn't need
to. I would remember.

The attendants all wore the same dress that stuck out
at the corners like the edges of a kite. They blended into
the matching blue airplane chairs and beige paneling. Blue
and beige, blue and beige.

"You're in 14A, a window," the attendant said, and
motioned to a row of seats. "I can take your bag."

I held it tight, feeling the hard cover of my journal,
the box of Chiclets, the can of guava juice Mamá Juanita
gave me, all my important things. "No. *Gra*— Thank
you."

"Okay," she looked down at my ticket stub, "Maria,
would you like something to drink? Apple juice, orange
juice, coffee, tea, water, soda—Coke, ginger ale, or Fanta?"
Her voice was twangy; the words blended together, like
saying the rosary.

Apple juice made my stomach turn. I wasn't thirsty
yet anyhow, and when I was, I could take care of myself.

"I've got this." I pulled the can from my bag and shook it.

She smiled. She wasn't exactly like all the other American attendants. Her hair, pinned back beneath her blue bonnet, was honey-colored, and her eyes, big and bright, were green like mine.

"Looks like you're ready to go." She winked. "I'm Cindy. If you need anything, just buzz." She pressed a button on the arm of the chair, and a light above my head flashed on like the morning star.

The seat smelled of old *café* and mouthwash. It was hard to get comfortable. The metal parts poked through the fabric, like bones through skin, so I used the small pillow for an extra seat cushion. It helped, and made it easier to see out the window.

Just before Cindy came around to check our safety belts, a woman with dark skin and flippy brown hair sat beside me. She wore blue jeans and a tight pink shirt, and her eyebrows formed two plucked arches that made her look like she'd just swallowed a bug, even when she smiled. She was American—pretty. But she smelled like *sofrito*. Like onions, peppers, capers, garlic. Like Mamá's kitchen.

She fastened her belt and pulled a *Vogue* magazine from her bag, then turned and asked, "You all by yourself?"

"*Sí*," I said, making my voice loud and sure. "I'm going to Washington, D.C."

"*La capitál*. Never been. I live in New York City," she explained.

"My teacher—Señora Alonzo—she's from there."

"Ah." She raised a brow higher. "You should come. There are many Puerto Ricans."

She opened her magazine. "I just came back to visit my sister. She's the only one left on the island."

I thought of Mamá and Papi, Mamá Juanita and Naranja, Tío Benny and Titi Ana, Titi Lola, Teline, Delia, and Pepito, and all my other family, great-*tíos* and -*titis*, second, third, and fourth cousins, the whole *barrio* of Florilla. I couldn't imagine not having family in Puerto Rico.

Out the window, the mountains seemed nothing more than a rolling line across the horizon. My gaze ran the crest, searching, but I was too far from our pink house. It was hidden beneath the spiked palms and Flamboyán trees of Borínquen.

As the plane took off, the woman read her magazine. I chewed my gum and prayed that angels would lift me into the air. I knew Angela was one of them. Through the window, I searched the sky for her. Puffs of white gave way to a sunny blue. My eyes ached at the brightness. I had to look away from the face of God. He was watching. He knew my story.

Like the emerald parrot, I soared high while far below, Papi, Mamá, and my island grew small. The blue, blue sea swallowed the green mountaintop until it was no more than a speck, a sesame seed floating in the darkness, and then nothing. The moment it disappeared, the sun's warmth seemed to empty from my body. Yet, for the first time, I knew for certain who I was.

The pilot announced that our flight time was three hours, forty-eight minutes, and that Washington, D.C., had snow flurries in the forecast. I curled my sandaled toes and pulled Mamá Juanita's sweater over my shoulders, soft and light. Snow. I remembered Mamá and Papi shaving balls of ice for my birthday *piraguas*, their faces warm and laughing. A Puerto Rican snowfall.

# Acknowledgments

I would like to thank Sheri Reynolds for believing in me before I fully believed in myself and for giving me the opportunity to follow my heart. I am forever grateful. I thank Janet Peery for setting the bar high and never allowing me to slip beneath it; Dr. Jeffrey Richards, for his never-ending encouragement and for saying, "I told you so"; my classmates in the MFA program for their insightful thoughts that weighted my pen; my trusted readers and lifelong friends Christy Fore, Stacy Rich, Sandra Scofield, and all those who loved me through long writing hermit spells.

To my agent, Doris Michaels, and my director of development, Delia Berrigan Fakis, I am enormously grateful for their continual support, warmth, and wisdom; my editor, Kate Kennedy, what can I say, you're amazing; Shaye Areheart and everyone at Shaye Areheart Books, thank you for believing in me and this story.

I could not possibly have written this novel without its fundamental inspiration, my family. To all of my extended family and especially my grandparents in Puerto Rico, Wilfredo Norat-Torres and Maria Esparra-Rivera, my love is immeasurable, and I hope I bring honor to our family's name and land. To my parents, Eleane and Curtis McCoy, you are my best friends and all that I strive to be. Thank you for seeing my gifts early and nurturing them. I am a writer because of you. To my brothers, Jason and Andrew, how could I have written of adolescence without the influence of my sidekicks? As men, you hold my esteem like no others.

Thank you to my husband, Brian Waterman, without whom I would certainly be lost. For your infinite support and patience during the writing of this book (and for forgiving the harrowing citrus-throwing incident), I promise a lifetime of Miss Ellen's Muffins and all my love.

Finally, I must say that I am grateful and immeasurably humbled by the work of the divine in my life. I count every breath and word as a blessing.

## About the Author

Sarah McCoy has taught writing at Old Dominion University and the University of Texas at El Paso. She lives with her husband in El Paso, Texas, where she is working on her second novel. Please visit www.SarahMcCoy.com.

# Discussion Guide

1. What role does food play in Puerto Rican culture? How does McCoy use specific foods to bring the characters together?

2. What kind of narrative voice has McCoy chosen for this novel? How do we connect with Verdita's character through that narrative style? How does the child's point of view enhance or detract from the book's impact?

3. Freud's theory of the primal scene asserts that when a child is faced with the sudden awareness of his or her parents' sexuality and intimacy, it shocks the psyche and sets the child's libido into motion. How do you see this affecting Verdita in chapter 1 and throughout the novel?

4. The discovery of identity is a common theme in coming-of-age (*bildungsroman*) stories. At the beginning of the book, Verdita's persona is directly tied to her parents. Finding her identity requires her to recognize the separation between who they are as a unit (Venusa and Faro) and who she is as an individual. Simultaneously, she battles with who her parents are in the intimate setting (Mamá and Papi) and who they are in public (Monaique and Juan); who she is in private (Verdita) and in

public (Maria~Flores). Discuss this and other social dualities Verdita faces in her coming~of~age struggle.

5. How is Verdita's coming of age in 1960s Puerto Rico different from a girl coming of age in America during that same period? How are they similar?

6. How have the Taino Indians and the indigenous island cul~ ture adapted to each of its colonizers (the Spanish and Ameri~ cans) and the African slaves brought by them? How do you see each of these influences in the novel? How does this compare to America's "melting pot" identity?

7. Much of Puerto Rican and other Latino fiction focuses on themes of migration to New York, Chicago, Miami, or other Latin~populated cities. How is this story different? How is it sim~ ilar? Discuss what you've learned about the island culture that you didn't know before reading the book. How is this culture dif~ ferent from the Puerto Rican immigrants in the United States?

8. At the beginning of chapter 3, Papi discusses Puerto Rico's possible statehood. Do you believe Puerto Rico should be a part of the United States? If so, why and what benefits does state~ hood offer? If not, why and what detriments come with it? Would it affect Puerto Rico's identity in a good or bad way?

9. A magical worldview is a common characteristic of the Latino culture. While McCoy's storytelling is more realistic,

how and where do you see elements of magic in the characters' lives?

10. What is the role of myth and story in Puerto Rican culture? How does it influence both individuals and the community?

11. Verdita believes in God, but her understanding of Him and how the supernatural interacts with the mortal is perplexing. The magical tales of the church mingle with the ones told within her family, the ones of Puerto Rico's heritage and history, and those of America. Many of the overlapping concepts contradict one another. For example, in the novel: Is there a king of the ocean or a God in heaven; would one make seashell wishes or prayers at the altar; is there a Santa Claus or Three Kings? In what other areas does Verdita struggle to find truth? Can you reconcile these conflicting truths?

12. The Greeks described love as a three-pronged fork. One prong is the fundamental emotion of compassion: *philia, storge,* and *agape* (cherishing, belonging, and self-sacrificing). The Greeks contended that upon coming of age and the budding of sexuality love branches into two additional prongs: *eros* and *epithumia* (romance and desire). How does McCoy portray philia, storge, and agape in the novel? How does she portray eros and epithumia?

13. Gender roles are addressed in the novel's text and subtext. What are the Puerto Rican gender roles in the home? What

are they in public? How do these compare with the projected American gender roles?

14. Patriarchy is a traditional characteristic of many Latino families. How do you see the Santiago family following in that tradition? How do you see them diverging from it? How does Verdita view femininity (represented by Mamá, Delia, Mamá Juanita, Titi Lola, the *puta* in San Juan) and masculinity (represented by Papi, Omar, Blake, Naranja)?

15. How is sexuality portrayed throughout the novel? Are women encouraged to embrace their sexuality or shun it? Discuss the conversation between Verdita and Mamá on page 121. How does Verdita deal with her sexuality and the sexuality of those around her? How does religion influence this?

16. Duality of culture is a major theme in McCoy's novel. How does American culture impact the traditional Puerto Rican society? How does it affect the language, the foods, the religion, the traditional gender roles of men and women, and so on?

17. In the end, after Verdita evaluates both the good and bad of life in America, why do you think she still chooses to leave her homeland? What brings her to this decision? What do you think Verdita will find when she lands in the United States— will her expectations be met? Will she be disappointed?

## Note on the Type

This book was set in Pastonchi MT, an oldstyle serif typeface, manufactured by Monotype. It was designed by Francesco Pastonchi (1877–1953), an Italian poet and author, with assistance from Professor Eduardo Cotti of the Royal School of Typography in Torino.